NIGHTWALKER 8

NIGHTWALKER 8

WRITTEN BY CRAIG MARTELLE, CREATED BY

FRANK RODERUS

LMBPN

DISRUPTIVE IMAGINATION

NIGHTWALKER 8 TEAM

Thanks to our Beta Readers

Micky Cocker, Dr. Jim Caplan, Kelly O'Donnell, and John Ashmore

Thanks to our JIT Readers

Peter Manis
Kelly O'Donnell
John Ashmore
Jeff Goode
Micky Cocker

Editor
Lynne Stiegler

CHAPTER ONE

"We need to wash these blankets," Wolfe muttered, rolling over and patting the bed where his wife was supposed to be.

It was dark; he had slept the whole day. Exhaustion had seized him in its merciless grip. He was stiff and still tired, but when he sat up and looked around, his brief confusion cleared away, leaving him with profound sadness. For the first time in as long as he could remember, he was sleeping in his bed, but he was alone.

Lurleen was missing. JoJo was not there, either, but he knew where they had gone. He removed the note from his pocket and carefully unfolded it.

Jim,

I hope you get this. JoJo and I were told to evacuate. None of the cars work so we had to walk. He is strong, and we will be fine. We are supposed to be going to Jacksonville. Please join us there as soon as you can.

I love you with all my heart.

L.

And Miss Jennifer was in Mobile with her dog Buddy.

"I never did like the heat down this way," he said to his empty home. "At least I do not have to pay the mortgage."

He joked because it was something that Lurleen would have laughed at. He missed her blonde hair and smile. He was wasting time, but he needed to eat. Yesterday's run had probably cost him a couple of pounds he did not have to lose. Wolfe rummaged through his kitchen before going to his shed out back. He was surprised to find it still locked, although he should not have been. He had built it out of concrete blocks, steel I-beams, and rebar. It was not big, but it was industrial-strength.

The combination lock on it still worked. Lurleen's birthday was the combination—8-2-73, although he had set it at 8-27-3. He spun the dial back and forth to the numbers, and it popped. The door squealed open on rusted hinges.

Inside, Wolfe found his lawnmower and trimmer, as well as gasoline and his dirt bike. Tools hung from a punchboard lining one of the walls. Two cases of home-canned food stood on the shelves. Half of them had popped, but the other half were good, including green beans, tomatoes, and even some venison. He gingerly set those aside and rolled the dirt bike onto the back porch.

Wolfe took stock of his supplies. Better to eat well tonight and head out tomorrow on the motorcycle, if he could get it running. This was a small two-fifty, but if the wheels were intact, the valves weren't rusted shut, and he could clear the carburetor, he could use it to save himself a great deal of grief.

He went into the house to get a pen and paper. His firepit was overgrown, but there were some old logs that he hoped would still catch fire. Using the paper as tinder, he lit a match and set the wood around it. A hand axe from his shed helped him make short work of a log, splitting it into kindling. Once the fire was going, he dumped a pound of meat and a jar of green beans into the pot.

In the kitchen, he took one of the only spices that wasn't in a single clump—red pepper flakes. He beat a salt shaker on the ground to break up some of it, enough to sprinkle in with his dinner. While it simmered, he braced the bike and brought out the tools he would need to fix it. His mind focused on how close they were, only an eight- to ten-hour drive away.

Wolfe stopped and hung his head. It had always been *only* one more thing, but that did not matter. He would keep doing one more thing after one more thing as long as there was one more to do.

Dinner was sizzling and popping, so he turned away from the bike and pulled the pan from the fire. He ate at the table like he always used to do, but in this changed world, he ate straight out of the pan. Lurleen would not have gone for that.

Wolfe ate in silence and quickly because he had work to do. The sooner he fixed the bike, the sooner he would be on the road to Jacksonville.

CHAPTER TWO

He tickled the throttle and jumped down on the starter, and the bike turned over but did not catch. Wolfe did not have a can of ether to goose it and give it that extra pop, so he lifted up and let his body weight cycle the starter. The bike belched a cloud of blue smoke as if running on a single cylinder. Wolfe played with the choke, then eased off. He gave the hand throttle a little twist, and the familiar whine of the dirt bike made him smile. He shut it down.

Wolfe tossed his tools back into the shed and put the cans of venison in his pack. He locked the shed behind him, although he was not sure why.

He threw his backpack on and made one last circuit of the house before rolling the bike in through the back door and out the front door. The yard was too overgrown to force his way through the gate. His car was still in the small garage, but EMP or something like that had killed the electronics. Cars were dead for thirty miles in every direction. It would not be an easy ride to get through, but it sure beat running.

He kickstarted the bike, and it purred as a dirt bike should. He gave it enough gas to get it rolling and headed down the street. It was barely past midnight, and he was able to ride without his goggles. Since his bike was not made for the street, it did not have a headlight. There was nothing to keep turned off.

Wolfe rode through the darkness, weaving through the junk on the streets. On the open highway, he was able to ride the shoulder line away from the majority of stalled vehicles, and in less than an hour, he made it to a more open road. He kicked the bike through the gears, squinting into the wind and letting his long hair flow. He ran it up to fifty but refused to go faster. He could not have the tires come apart at speed. Even with his incredible strength, he might not survive the crash. He had come too far to fail now.

He needed his tank of gas to get him as far as it could, and the bike had not been driven in four years. Any mile he could get out of it was one less mile he had to run, so he backed it down to thirty-five and cruised easily. Even at that speed, he would make it before dawn.

Wolfe could only think of Lurleen and JoJo and what could have happened to them. Had they made it to the camp outside Jacksonville or diverted to somewhere else?

He had left home a long time ago to work as an over-the-road truck driver. He had been on a road through Idaho with a load of nutrition bars and freeze-dried foods when he saw the explosions in the distance. He knew what they were, so he'd found an old mine and, working like there would be no tomorrow, he'd carried his load inside one box at a time until he feared the radiation would sweep across the land outside.

Wolfe had remained underground in the dark for two years, surviving on nothing but the food he'd pulled off his truck and water from a pool in the depths of the cave. When he finally ran out of food, he emerged into the daylight. He found that he could no longer tolerate the sun. His hair had turned white, and he had the strength of ten men. He could also sense the radiation; a tingle in his fingers told him of its presence.

That awareness and strength had saved him over the years since. Once he'd found the welding goggles, he could stand the daylight, too. It had been a long four years since he had last seen Lurleen and JoJo. He hoped it had not been the last time, that thought being the worst of the trials he faced.

We never know the last time we do things: the last time we run outside as a child to play with our friends, the last time we say "I love you," the last time we see someone. The movie of Jim Wolfe's life played in his mind. He'd saved the dog who had joined him on the road to Florida. Jennifer's father had saved him but had later taken his own life after the mother died. Jennifer had joined Wolfe, too.

There was little good in the world that had survived the bombs, but it was starting to take root and flourish in areas like Mobile. He sped up, feeling that now was the time to bring this chapter of his existence to an end. He would find Lurleen or confirm that she had not made it.

His breath caught as he thought about it. If she had not survived the new world, JoJo would not have made it either.

The thought grated on his soul but didn't darken it like a cancer. He had the brightness of his adopted daughter and the German Shepherd to hold the darkness at bay. He drove on, squinting into the wind.

CHAPTER THREE

With the early morning came the dewy chill, enhanced by the motorcycle's speed. At Gainesville, Wolfe left Interstate 75 and headed east on Highway 24 on his way to 301 to take him straight into Jacksonville. He worked his way through the wreckage littering the city, finally reaching the far side. He stopped to fix himself something to eat. The long run from the day prior continued to sap his energy. He did not want to collapse the second he arrived.

Since the bombs, nothing had come as easy as it could. The war had made everything hard, even what should have been simple, like getting from one point on the map to another. As a truck driver, he had done it all day, every day.

In a small building that had been looted, Wolfe found kindling and made a fire. He took his one frying pan out of his pack and poured in a pound of venison and a jar of tomatoes. He had brought the salt and pepper flakes because he had eaten enough unseasoned food to last a lifetime.

The little things brought back a life closer to normal. He sat in the darkness, the small fire crackling with a frying pan on top of it, filled with his dinner. Wolfe ate in silence. He had been alone for a long time, and now he was alone again. He decided he preferred company.

He finished eating and cleaned up quickly. The night was getting old, and he had a few miles left to go. Wolfe thought he could make it in an hour, getting there before dawn so he could find the camp before the daylight cost him his advantage.

Night was his close companion. He could see with the welding goggles on, but it was greatly limited. He needed to have a plan before he started searching a large group of people.

He was not beyond yelling for Lurleen and JoJo.

He held his breath as he kicked the bike to life, exhaling after it started, then eased onto the road and accelerated. Thirty miles passed in a flash. His excitement grew despite his best efforts to tamp it down, trying to throw water on what was threatening to be a blazing fire.

A light in the distance stilled his racing heart. He shut the bike off and coasted up the road, craning his neck to see what lay ahead. The bike slowed until it stopped, then he jumped off, ran to the nearest rusted wreck, and leaned his nearly pristine dirt bike against it. He headed closer to the heavily overgrown ditch on his side of the four-lane road. Wolfe only needed to keep from silhouetting himself.

If this were a checkpoint, something he expected close to the camp, any guards would be night-blind from their own lights. The darkness was his friend, not theirs.

He loped soundlessly up the road, feeling his boots on his feet and happy to have them. There was a fire on the cross-road between the two lanes. Wolfe stayed far enough away that he could block the light with his hand while looking around it for those who had lit it.

A sound came from his left, and he crouched and

searched the area. He heard the crunch of a footfall someone was trying to silence, so he backed slowly into the undergrowth. From behind a wreck ahead, two men walked carefully, carrying shotguns. "I heard a motorcycle," one whispered harshly. "A dirt bike. I have not forgotten what those sound like."

The young man sounded like he was used to not being believed.

Wolfe waited, but they were sniffing around and would eventually find the motorcycle. These men were in his way, and they carried shotguns. He rushed from the edge of the trees, grabbing both shotguns while ramming one of the two, knocking him down. Wolfe moved to the side to avoid highlighting himself against the fire in the distance.

"Hell!" The man still standing waved his arms around, trying to find his attacker, but Wolfe now had both shotguns. He tossed one into the heaviest clump of trees, and the splash when it hit told him that it would not be operable in a couple days because of the inevitable rust.

He looked at the second shotgun to make sure he could fire it if needed. The man on the ground moaned. The other kicked him as he moved closer, almost falling on top of his fellow guard.

With his hands as his guide, he helped the other to his feet.

"Who's there?" one called with a measure of bravado. "I think a deer hit me."

"Yeah, I heard a splash where it was running through the brush. We need to find those shotguns."

The two dropped to their knees and started patting the ground in an expanding semicircle as they searched almost frantically for their weapons.

Wolfe had options: eliminate the men, ignore them and drive past, or give up the bike and walk to maintain his anonymity. But what if they had information that could help him?

His trusting nature kicked in. "You are not going to find your shotguns because I took them," he said from far enough away that they could not rush him. He had learned a great deal in the last four years—the hard way.

"Who's there? Is that you, Billy?" one man called, reaching toward Wolfe as he stood. Jim tiptoed to the side to avoid being where they thought he was. "Stop messing around."

"I do not think that is Billy," the second suggested. "What do you want, Mister?"

"I want information, that is all. I do not want to hurt anyone."

"Hurting us is in your hands. Not sure how you can see us since it is black as pitch out here." The man shuffled his feet, tensing. "Or maybe you can't."

He rushed toward where he thought Wolfe was, and Jim kicked his legs out from under him. He went palms-first into the pavement, followed by smashing his face into it. He grunted and whined, rolling over. His hands were torn up from the fall.

"You might want to clean those scratches out, once you tell me what I want to know." Wolfe stepped away again, but the younger man was rooted to the ground. Even a strong wind would not have moved him. "Where is the refugee camp?"

"There is a big one about fifteen miles straight ahead, just east of Baldwin," the young man answered while the other told him to shut up.

"How many people are in the camp?"

"I dunno, Mister. A lot. Maybe twenty thousand? I cannot say for sure." The young man became nervous. The other remained on the ground, holding his hands out and breathing raggedly. "Why do you want to know?"

"I think my wife and young son are in there, and I aim to find them."

"Good luck," the young man blurted before slapping a hand over his mouth. "Do not kill me, but you have a hard road ahead, even if you are able to speak with the commandant."

Wolfe shook his head and took his time before replying. "I am not a fan of fancy titles. If he knows the answers to any of my questions, then I will ask him. I will ask every single person there until I get my answer. Tell me about the camp. How does it run?"

The other man worked his way to his feet and shuffled forward to bump into the younger guard. "Shut up, I told you!"

Wolfe stepped forward, ramming the butt of the shotgun into the man's gut. He doubled over and collapsed, hitting the roadway with a heavy thud.

"I asked you a question. Please, tell me." Wolfe was starting to lose patience. He clenched his jaw at the realization that he was willing to kill these men and willed the feeling away. That would not make him worthy of his family. These men were doing a job they had been told to do. Do not fight the rattles, cut the head off the snake, and that removes the danger. He needed to find the ones giving orders and deal with them.

"The camp is mostly women, a few men, and no children. That is why I did not want to say, Mister. Your kid ain't there."

"Where did they send the families?"

"That is just it. They sent the children to a second camp north of J-ville. There are no families."

Wolfe leaned close to the young man, stomping on the other's hand when he reached out. "There will always be families, even if they are not together. I think that is something I am going to have to remedy. I cannot tolerate men with power enslaving the good people of this country. They only want to get on with their lives and provide for their families. Who thinks he has the right to take that away?"

"The commandant," the young man said, barely above a whisper.

The man on the ground started reaching out again, this time with the other hand. "I have had enough of you." He reared back and kicked the man in the head, and the sharp crack of a breaking neck said he was never getting up again.

"What is your name?"

"My name is Seth, Seth Hammerlin. The commandant is Elric Pardone. The man on the ground is his son Eldon. Was…"

"I can already tell that I will not like this Elric. I think it is time for a change of commandant. What do you say?"

"I dunno, Mister. What should I say?"

"That you want to come along and be part of the change?" Wolfe offered.

"I do not think that is for me." He looked at the ground, even though he could not see it in the dark, and shuffled his feet, seeking a pebble to kick.

"I cannot have you telling the commandant about me. Not for a couple days, at least."

"Please, do not kill me. I can make myself scarce, easy. There is a fishing boat not far from here."

"You have saved your life," Wolfe replied before spinning around and tossing the shotgun into the brush. "Are there any more checkpoints between here and Baldwin?"

"Two, I think. The guards set up where they want, so I cannot tell you exactly where they are."

"Much obliged. Now, do us both a favor and make yourself scarce."

"What about the commandant's son?"

"You do not need to worry about him. Go on. Get out of here."

"Yes sir, Mister... Mister... What's your name?"

"Go on before you make me mad." Wolfe had a different agenda for this trip. He did not want to let them know he was coming. The commandant did not matter to him except for the potential knowledge he had regarding Lurleen. Surprise would give him a slight advantage if the commandant was not waiting for him.

Lurleen! I am coming for you. He had a feeling she was there. He did not know why or how, but that did not matter. His gift for sensing radiation worked. There was no reason to question it, either.

Wolfe picked up the body by the feet and spun it around until he built enough momentum to send it winging into the brush, splashing down in the same area as the shotguns.

With renewed confidence, Wolfe hurried back to his motorcycle, kicked it to life, and raced past Seth on his way to Baldwin.

CHAPTER FOUR

Less than ten miles later, Wolfe came across the next checkpoint. He stopped short of it, like last time.

Figuring going farther would push his luck, he chose stealth. He pushed his bike back along the highway until he found a side road, where he hauled the motorcycle into an overgrown backyard to hide it in an ancient shed that was halfway to falling down, a place people were done looking for something good to scavenge.

Wolfe tried to fix the grass that he had squashed, managing to get it somewhat back in shape. It was Florida, so in a few days, any sign that he had been there would be gone. He had no idea if he would come back this way. The bike was an option, nothing more. It had served its purpose.

He jogged back to the main road and started to run. False dawn was near, so he needed to make good time to get a look at the camp while it was still dark. He stopped when he realized where he was. It was a little town short of I-10 and Baldwin. There had been road construction, and they had detoured him around it. He faded into nearby Maxwell, little more than a small number of residences wrapped around a few businesses, all defunct in the new world.

Wolfe bypassed the checkpoint, making his way out of the hamlet and onto the back road he had driven one time. He followed it to a crossroad that went north to Baldwin, took that, and started running. With the arrival of the pre-dawn brightening, he veered onto the shoulder to blend with the overgrowth should someone be watching from up ahead.

But there was no one there.

He had a straight shot to the town and the other side of the interstate, the area where he thought a camp would be since it had huge warehouses and wide fields where they used to run dairy cattle. He expected none of that to still be in operation. He hurried ahead, stopping when he heard a hammer draw back, making a distinctive click. He had heard the sound too often over the past four years. He froze and slowly raised his hands.

"What do we have here? Looks like a wraith, don't you think, Frankie?"

"I'm Billy, wearing a wig that I found out there. I thought you would like it."

"Billy?" You are not due on shift for a while, so what were you doing down there?"

"Nothing much. Out for a walk, that's all." Wolfe slowly turned, lowering his hands at the same time.

"You take it easy! Don't be sneaking up on us like that."

"Sorry, guys." Wolfe stepped closer. "Got a light?"

"You found smokes? Good ones? I ain't carried a lighter since we ran out of smokes three years ago. What are you smoking, Billy?"

"The good stuff," Wolfe laughed until he was close enough to hammer a fist into the pistol-holder's face. He jumped across the falling body to deliver an uppercut to the second

man's chin, lifting him off the ground. He fell back, unconscious before he hit the ground.

Wolfe took the pistol and hurried away. They had not
seen what he looked like besides his white hair. He had run
out of dye a long time ago. That meant he could continue
into the day after scouting the camp now.

He ran down the road toward Baldwin, slowing after half
a mile when traffic appeared on the interstate: people
walking and horse-drawn wagons. He heard the creak of
leather harness and squeak of modern axles under blue-tarp-
covered wooden prairie schooners.

Wolfe walked under the interstate, then jogged north to
catch the highway that led to the camp.

There was no way Wolfe could miss it. The guard towers
on the corners made it look like a prison. Armed men in the
turrets convinced him that they were up to no good.
Highway 90 led into the area between two heavily fenced
and razor-wired facilities. A building had been erected, and
Wolfe thought they had done it since the bombs fell.

He believed it was the only newly constructed building he
had run across in the past four years. He expected to find the
commandant in such a place, but it was early, despite the
activity. Then again, it was Florida in the late summer, and
there was no air conditioning. Physical activity needed to
happen before the sun delivered enough heat to kill the
unprotected and unaware.

Wolfe pulled his welding goggles over his eyes. It was
bright enough that he could no longer see without squinting
while holding his hand in front of his face. The world dark-
ened to a hazy dark gray.

Wolfe strolled between the two areas, noting that the vast
majority of those inside were women. They were dressed up
to some extent, making them look less like prisoners.

"Can I help you?" a man carrying a rifle said. He moved in front of Wolfe to block his way.

"I am looking for work. New in town and trying to make my way."

"Why do you think there is work to be had here?"

"Because there is," Wolfe stated. He was not in a mood for a verbal standoff. Leaders drunk on their own power always had room for strong people to support them. "I believe in what the commandant is doing. I want to show my support in a more practical way."

The man snorted. "Fine. Follow me."

Wolfe was gratified that the man gave in so quickly. He did not have another play besides going away and raiding the place during the dark of night. Since he could walk in the front door, he chose that option. He might still come back later, but then he would know the layout of the building and have more information about the guards and processes.

Inside, a number of women worked at desks, heads down as they sorted through papers, making annotations, transferring information to ledgers, and tallying and creating new reports. None of them looked up.

They walked through the area, with Wolfe's escort tracing a finger along each woman's arm as they passed. He noted that they did not flinch or react in any way.

Wolfe's anger built. He calmed himself to keep from launching into a rage. There were six others with guns standing along the outside walls of the room. They went through another room that looked comparable before reaching the stairs to the second floor. Wolfe had seen at least three doors leading outside. On the second floor, the décor changed to thick throw rugs, color on the walls, a minimum of furniture, and air conditioning.

"Stay here. You can sit." He pointed to a loveseat pushed into an alcove.

Wolfe did as he was directed. There would be a time for standing up to this crew, but it was not now.

The escort sat on the corner of the pretty receptionist's desk. She smiled and batted her eyelashes while fighting off the man's wandering hands. Wolfe appreciated her deft touch in playing the game but refusing to become a ready victim of it. She rolled her chair back and smoothly escaped through oak doors into an office beyond.

"Be ready. If the commandant agrees to see you, you'll get two minutes to plead your case." The man waited with one cheek parked on the receptionist's desk. When she reappeared, she held the door for them, standing behind it in such a way as to keep it as a barrier between her and the escort.

But he remained outside. "The commandant will see you now. Remember what I told you," he added, loud enough for everyone to hear.

Wolfe made sure to walk between him and the receptionist. Keeping his hands where she could see them, he spoke softly as he passed. "Thank you kindly, ma'am." He did not try to look at her, focusing on the office ahead and the heavyset man behind the massive dark-wood desk.

There was a nameplate on the desk that read Mister Pardone. The man waved Wolfe forward, and Jim took in the office as he entered. Two grossly oversized men were sitting in the corners of the room, and both stood as soon as Wolfe entered. The commandant chuckled.

"Thank you for agreeing to see me, Mister Pardone," Wolfe said softly. "My name is Jim Wolfe, and I am looking for work."

"Be straight with me, Wolfe. Are you here because of the women?"

"I do not know what you mean. I have my own woman

back in Mobile, but life is hard. I want a roof over my head, food in my stomach, and the means to earn both of those."

"Ah. That might make you different from everyone else here, but what are your skills? There is no work for yet another jack-of-all-trades."

"I am very strong," Wolfe offered.

"Ha!" the commandant blurted. He gestured to one of the big men, who strolled forward with a lopsided grin spread across his face and thrust out his hand. Wolfe took it and squeezed with all the immense strength in his arm. The big man cried out and collapsed to his knees.

"I think he broke my hand!"

"Get out," the commandant told the man. "Go see the doc and send Binford in here."

"Yes, sir, Mister Pardone," the man replied in the voice of a sycophant, glaring at Wolfe while he stood.

"There is more of that if you want," Wolfe snarled at the man, who was trying not to be obvious about cradling his injured hand.

These men understood power. Wolfe had just given them a demonstration. Only alpha dogs ran with this pack, and Wolfe was not going to play second fiddle to a lackey.

The commandant chuckled anew. "I have never seen anything so profound. I can use a man who is stronger than every other man, Wolfe, but do I have your loyalty?"

"I believe loyalty is earned. You are in charge of all of this, so you must be doing something right." It was not a direct answer. The only thing Wolfe wanted was to find Lurleen and get the hell out of there.

The man who'd escorted Wolfe appeared, hurrying in front of the desk in response to his summons.

"Get Wolfe set up. He will not get to carry a weapon until he has proven himself, but he is well on his way." The commandant examined Jim Wolfe from head to toe. "What is with those goggles?"

"Sensitive to light. Had it my whole life, just like the hair," Wolfe lied.

Binford spoke up. "Yes, Mister Pardone. Any particular work you have in mind for him?"

"Right here, Binford. The music has stopped, and there seems to be an empty chair. Wolfe can fill it. For now."

Binford tried not to let his distaste show. "Of course, Mister Pardone."

He waved for Wolfe to follow him out.

To the side of the receptionist, a plain door led to a break room that doubled as a locker room. "Put your trash in here and get back in the commandant's office. I do not know what you did to get inside so quickly, but I will keep my eyes on you." He stabbed a finger into Wolfe's chest to emphasize his point.

Wolfe stared at the finger until Binford took it away. "Your lack of faith in Mister Pardone's decision-making is problematic. How much trouble do you want to make? I only want to earn my keep. I am not here for your job or his. I just want a roof over my head and something to eat. Is that too much to ask?"

Binford huffed and stormed away.

Wolfe strode after him, returning to the commandant's office and taking a seat opposite the other bodyguard. Jim Wolfe sat in silence for the next two hours while Pardone read one report after another, dutifully delivered by the receptionist. She glanced his way, taking in the new guard, but he refused to make eye contact.

He had no designs on anyone except Lurleen, and maybe the receptionist would know where to look. He needed to earn her trust to even ask the question.

CHAPTER FIVE

By lunchtime, Wolfe was hungry again. He had expended a great deal of energy to get where he was. He had also been up since the night before. Now he was close and fighting the other distractions to keep his focus. It would not do to ruin the opportunity.

Pardone was not one to eat at his desk. He stood, stretched, and walked out without a word to his bodyguards. Wolfe's counterpart across the room rushed after him. Wolfe followed, wondering if he had been hired as his personal security.

Wherever the commandant went, was he supposed to follow?

He would do what the other guard did until he was told something different.

They followed Pardone down the stairs and to the back of the building. Before going outside, the commandant donned a wide-brimmed hat of the type beachgoers used to wear. He removed his suit jacket and hung it on a hook by the door.

"Hungry?" he asked before laughing. "I can hear your stomach growling from the other side of the building."

"Just trying to earn my keep before I get fed, Mister Pardone."

"Keep that attitude, Wolfe. I need men who think of their job before themselves. That is what made this country great and will again! You are in for a treat. You will get something after I've partaken. We start early, nap often, and stay late. It is how we keep this business going."

"Thank you for sharing your wisdom, Mister Pardone."

Wolfe was dying to ask what the business was, but then his bluff to Binford would be laid bare. He had another day, maybe two before Pardone's son's disappearance would be discovered since that was when Seth would return. If the commandant brought him into the office for an interrogation, he might recognize Wolfe, but then again, he might not. If Jim spoke, it would confirm that it was him.

He needed to be done with what he needed to do by the end of tomorrow. The clock was ticking. He was closer to being able to ask the question—maybe too close. He had no freedom to ask anything, even under the guise of wanting to understand the business to better fill his role in it. If only he knew what the business was.

They walked across the path and along a road that led into the middle of the prison compound. Wolfe could think of no other way to describe it. Some women came up to the fence to deliver hollow accolades to the commandant, who waved them away as if they were bothering him.

At the end of the drive was a barn where the dairy products used to be processed. As they got closer, Wolfe could smell it. The farm was still active, and cattle roamed somewhere nearby. Maybe the women worked the pastures and fields between dressing up and trying to look good. Their existence was purchased with the labor of their bodies. Wolfe cast furtive glances into the fenced areas on both sides.

Prisons punishing those who had not done anything

wrong. Wolfe had been counting the number of men with rifles. Dozens of them. Would they fight for Pardone if he was gone? That was a question Wolfe would not be able to answer until it happened. His dislike for the man grew with each moment of disdain he showed those he kept caged.

The house on the old farm had been turned into an estate with the highest level of opulence that could be achieved in the hard times following the war.

More armed men stood around the house, nodding politely to the commandant as he passed. They eyed Wolfe suspiciously as a newcomer heading into the lord's manor. They did not like it one bit, but Wolfe ignored them. He had a job to do, and it was inside.

The other guard went in before Pardone.

Wolfe wondered if he had been ambushed in his own house before. After a quick "all clear," they walked inside.

Pardone's stride changed to a saunter as he gloated about his status and the wealth on display. Things of value had probably been looted from the surrounding area and put in the estate to lord over everyone else.

He finally made it to the dining room, where an obnoxiously long oak table was surrounded by matching high-backed chairs. Every place was set as if a dinner party would take place at any moment.

The commandant walked to the end, where he took his seat. The four servants in the room rushed to make him comfortable. The first guard took a place against the wall. Wolfe looked for his spot, but nothing was obvious. An empty corner behind Pardone seemed like it needed to be occupied. Wolfe headed there, but Pardone stopped him.

"No. Over there." He pointed toward the first guard. Wolfe immediately turned and went that way, taking the same stance as the other man.

The commandant did not want anyone behind him while

he ate. Even the servants worked from the front. It was okay for people to walk behind him when he was outside, but inside, his paranoia was on full display. His ego was stronger than his paranoia. Wolfe locked that tidbit away for later use, if necessary.

Food started to arrive. The servants put the dishes in front of Pardone and before the place to his left. Steak, with greens on the side as well as mashed potatoes and gravy.

"Where is she?" he asked. None of the servants knew, but one ran off. Wolfe remained stoic. The smell of the food made his stomach grumble even worse. It looked like an old-fashioned feast, the likes of which were rare in the current world.

The commandant unwrapped a linen-covered basket and removed a steaming bun. He took a bite and chewed slowly but didn't touch any of the other food.

"When we moved this conglomerate from the ways of the past to the ways of the present, Mister Wolfe, we encountered a significant labor shortage—those willing to work versus those willing to work for the greater good. All they needed was leadership to steer them in the right direction. My family has owned this farm since before I was born. I hope I have done my part in growing the business, making it something my great-granddaddy would be proud of.

"Although we all partake of the fruits of our lush pastures, we do have our favorites. I have been smitten. I know you are thinking that a man like me can pick and choose, but variety is the spice of life, is it not?"

Wolfe did not know if he was supposed to answer, but the silence and the look from Pardone cleared up his confusion.

"It is, Mister Pardone," Wolfe agreed.

"It is only natural," the commandant replied.

The door opened, and Pardone stood. *At least you learned some manners*, Wolfe thought.

Wolfe's heart leapt into his throat and pounded so hard he thought he would explode. Through the door walked Lurleen, magnificent in the graceful way she moved. His mouth fell open at the revelation that she was alive and well. He immediately snapped it shut when the two hugged and Pardone kissed her cheek.

"Take a seat, my dear. What held you up, the usual?" he asked pleasantly, even though he had not been pleased by being kept waiting.

"The workers need to be tended as much as the cattle." Lurleen's voice was like a crystal waterfall beneath a rainbow.

"Please try not to be late again."

"I could not come into your presence without cleaning up first. You deserve better than that." She looked around the room, her eyes locking on her husband, who stared back. She swallowed hard. "We have a new guest. Are you going to introduce me? Where are your manners, good sir?"

She forced a laugh and put her hand on his arm while never taking her eyes off Jim.

Wolfe vibrated with the tension coursing through his body. He could not focus. His mind raced with the possibilities. The image of delivering a great amount of violence to Elric Pardone's person pounded his mind from behind his eyes.

Eyes he could not close since Lurleen was alive!

"Introduce yourself and tell us about yourself," Pardone commanded, not leaving any room to doubt who was in charge and who followed the orders. The unspoken "be quick about it" came through loud and clear.

He took one step forward, clasping his hands before him while he looked down and started speaking. "I am honored to meet you, ma'am. My name is Jim Wolfe, and I come from the former state of Idaho. It has taken me all this time to get here, where I have found like-minded people willing to work hard for their families." He stepped back to demonstrate he was done.

"Wolfe might be the strongest man I ever met. That is the kind of person I want to work for me. Word is spreading, Lurleen. We are feeding the new world. The good we do is known across this once-great nation. We will make it great again!" The commandant spoke passionately, embracing what he was doing and that it was good because of the results. "Smells good, does it not?"

He gestured for her to sit down. Lurleen took her place and ate in silence, glancing at Wolfe when Pardone was not watching.

They finished their meal quickly, and he made to usher her out the door through which she had entered earlier. She stopped, placing her hand on his arm again. Wolfe steeled his expression.

"I need to thank the men who keep the commandant safe," she said with a twinkle in her eye and a smile. No one could refuse such a request. Ego persevered.

"Of course, my dear."

She faced Wolfe, and once again his heart raced. He could not control it. *Soon,* he promised with his eyes.

I love you, she mouthed. Pardone was looking over her shoulder.

"The pleasure is all mine, ma'am," Wolfe said out loud.

Lurleen shook his hand gently, delicately. It had a softness he faintly remembered. The blood coursed through his head, making him dizzy. He stood his ground firmly, doing his best not to waver. Lurleen moved to the next man and shook his hand before continuing the game by hugging Pardone and kissing his cheek before hurrying from the room.

"I saw you, Wolfe," the commandant said, strolling up to him.

I could kill you right now and no one could stop me, Wolfe thought. "Sir?"

"Any other woman is fair game. I saw you trying not to look at Sheila, my receptionist. Even she is available, all of them except Lurleen. She is mine and mine alone. No one horns in on my action."

"I would never deign to touch an angel, Mister Pardone. Look at me. I know my place."

"You know what, Wolfe? I actually believe you. Damn! You are moving up in this man's world." He looked at the big man, who was trying not to scowl. "You, too, Kleetus. You are good people. I am truly blessed. Grab your plates, and then I will go upstairs for a nap."

Kleetus elbowed Wolfe on his way to the table, taking the remaining steak and the rest of the mashed potatoes, leaving only the salad greens behind. He smiled when he turned. Wolfe still had not moved.

"It was mighty nice of you to fix Wolfe's plate. Add some greens and a bun or two, then give it to your partner." Pardone's voice was cold. The bodyguard's smile froze, but he did as ordered. Wolfe hurried up and halved what was there to dump on a second plate that he handed back. "That is how partners treat each other, and you will keep doing just that if you want to keep your head on your shoulders."

Pardone had not been talking to Wolfe. The other guard was appropriately chastised, while Wolfe remained stoic. He needed a completely new plan. He was no longer looking for information. He had learned what he had spent the last four years working to discover. The only question that remained was, "Where is JoJo?"

They moved to the hallway, where Pardone continued upstairs. His bodyguards were to stay at the bottom of the stairs, where they could eat while keeping anyone from going up.

Thoughts roiled Wolfe's mind, taking one hundred percent of his attention. The poke in his shoulder roused him to the moment.

"Did you hear me?" the other guard asked. "I said, we gotta stick together if we are going to make it. Next step up from here is foreman. We can both get there as long as we do not fight each other." He looked sincere.

"I have fought you and have no intention of doing so again."

The man's true colors had shown through, despite his earlier effort to win Wolfe over. "No kidding. I don't know what trick you pulled, but there is no way a skinny bastard like you could break someone's hand. You are not stronger than me."

"A trick, yes. I do not wish to fight you." That was true. Wolfe knew he could kill the man in a fair fight or even an unfair one. Wolfe was focused like a starving rattlesnake on a rabbit. He needed to rescue Lurleen. He'd promised to do it tomorrow, but how?

CHAPTER SIX

The end of the day came late, but there was plenty of light left. Wolfe was given access to the staff dining hall, not far from the main house. He was also given a small private room. All the guards had them for their recreational activities when they were off-shift.

Wolfe had seen it before in a town called Paradise, run by a woman of pure evil masquerading as a saint. It made him sick to his stomach, knowing that Lurleen was in such a place.

But she had survived by doing what she had to, as he had done.

He tried to sleep but could not. He finally got up around midnight and headed out, leaving his pack in his room. His door did not lock from the outside. Nothing in the compound locked except the master's house.

Nothing mattered to Wolfe except that Lurleen was in the big house. He headed out, goggles on in the dim lights of the bunkhouse. He ignored the noises from the other rooms as much as he could.

There was too much pain in that building. Only some of it was his.

What would Lurleen have him do? He knew the answer to that. She would not go unless everyone was able to walk free with her. And where was JoJo? Probably in the children's area. Lurleen had to believe he was okay, or a dark cloud would have hung over her head.

Wolfe stopped. He was awake and would not be able to rest until this was over. He returned to his room, shouldered his pack, and walked back outside, where he was enveloped by the darkness.

Once in the shadows, he removed the AR-15 from his pack, assembled it, and pocketed the magazines and the remainder of his ammunition. He stuffed the pistol he had taken into his belt. He decided to take on the house first and work his way outward. Cut the head off the snake. Upend their way of life.

He looked around to get his bearings. A quarter-mile away were the massive sheds that had once been the milking facility and now housed the facility's captives. Allies—an army ten thousand strong. He could not do this alone, but with Lurleen by his side, they could do right by everyone.

Wolfe kicked his pack into the brush. A single light shone upstairs. Would that be Pardone's bedroom? That choice seemed to be slightly better than his others. Around the outside of the house, guards roamed, but the dim lights did not help them see away from the building. Wolfe determined the pattern they paced, which was steady with consistent timing. They walked up to each other and then returned to the next guard. If Wolfe acted quickly enough, he could take out all six before they raised the alarm. He returned to his pack and removed his hunting knife.

With a pistol in one hand and his knife in the other, he stalked toward the manor house.

He waited until the two guards were at their farthest points and slunk in to melt into a nearby bush to wait for the guard to return. He pocketed the pistol and thrust the knife into his boot, then stepped from the bush and into the guard's footsteps. A quick lunge, and he had the man around his chin. With a violent twist, he wrenched his head around, snapping his neck. He dragged him back to the bush and dumped him in, taking his rifle and hat to maintain the façade. The clock was now ticking before the guards would stop running into their fellows.

Wolfe hurried up to catch up to where he was supposed to be when he ran into the next guard. He kept his head down. When he met the other guard, he stepped close and drove the heel of his hand into the man's nose, shattering the bones and sending shards into his brain. He left the body right there and started to run along the path the guard walked night after night.

The other guard was on his way back when Jim slowed to meet him, well into his routine.

"You are out of position. This is my sector," the man complained.

Wolfe mumbled something and staggered, dropping to his knees. His fellow guard rushed to him, only to die on the point of Wolfe's blade. Wolfe jumped up and continued running. He did not have time for much more subterfuge. He jogged erratically toward the next guard, delivering a weak cry for help.

Like the other man, he ran toward Wolfe, and like the other, he died quickly. Two left, and the alarm had not yet been raised. Wolfe sprinted as fast as his legs would carry him. The guard had his back turned, still looking for the other guard, who was probably at the end of his sector wondering where his counterpart was.

Wolfe body-blocked him from behind, pummeling him

into the ground and breaking his neck to make sure he wouldn't follow, then took off again. One last guard. He was walking toward him, not far from the front of the house, his rifle in his arms. He started to take aim. Wolfe threw his knife with all the power of his considerable strength.

The knife flashed in the night, hitting the guard butt-first in the middle of his forehead. His head snapped back while his body continued forward. Wolfe slid to a stop, straddling the man, but his caved-in forehead said he had not survived the attack. As Wolfe dragged him into nearby bushes, he thanked Florida for its heavy growth, making the hiding of bodies a much easier task. He tracked around the building to where the light was still on.

Wolfe did not waste time thinking about the meager power generation supplying the facility. Very few lights were on. Whatever was available was dedicated to the main building and the estate house. The commandant was provided for. Everyone else could do without.

Everyone else. The plan solidified in his mind, everything that needed to happen this night.

Wolfe closed on the house, using the ledges to crawl up and climb to the second floor. The strength in his fingers cracked the stucco and left marks of his passing, but it was a one-way trip. He had no intention of leaving by the same route.

Hanging from the window ledge. Wolfe pulled himself up to where he could see inside. There was a huge bed with two people in it. The light was on and Lurleen held a book before her, reading. It was her way. The lump under the covers next to her told him where the commandant was. Wolfe clung to the ledge with one hand and lightly tapped the window. Lurleen's head snapped sideways to look that way, and Wolfe waved to his wife.

She nodded and put the book down. She turned off the

light and slowly crawled out of the bed, then walked around it to unlock the window and slide it open.

"What are you doing?" Pardone grumbled.

"Stuffy in here. I need some fresh air," she said. "You go back to sleep, darling. I'll be beside you shortly." Lurleen's slight drawl would disarm even the most stalwart of men.

They waited for his breathing to slow before Wolfe pulled himself up and started scrambling inside. Lurleen coughed to cover the noise, turning to face Pardone to cough at him to make it even more profound, which did not have the effect she wanted.

He roused, blinking his eyes open. She stepped closer to the bed, blocking his view of the window. She leaned across him to grab her pillow, sliding it back toward her. Pardone tried to see around her. She moved quickly, jamming the pillow against his face and standing to put her body weight over it.

Pardone was too strong. He twisted her wrists off the pillow and pushed her hands and the pillow away from his mouth. "What the hell?" He sounded more surprised than angry.

"I slipped," she said innocently. Pardone saw the shadow behind her and recoiled at the flash of white hair.

Wolfe drove his fist into the commandant's face, bouncing his head off the wall before grabbing the big man by the throat and squeezing. Pardone started to thrash. Had the lights been on, they would have seen him turn blue. Wolfe half-picked him up by his throat and shook him as a dog might. The commandant started to gurgle as his windpipe was crushed beneath Wolfe's fingers.

Another shake to snap the unconscious man's neck and Wolfe deposited him on the bed, already forgotten as he turned to Lurleen.

She fell to her knees. "I am so sorry, Jim. I thought you were dead!"

Wolfe kneeled next to her and hugged her tightly. "You have nothing to be sorry for, you hear me? You did what you had to do to survive. You made it possible for us to be back together. If anyone is sorry, it is me for being away when the world came to an end. I got here as quickly as I could. I found your note in our house."

He smiled, and tears welled into his eyes. He had pulled his goggles down, and they were around his neck. She still couldn't see his eyes in the dark.

They had the same thought at the same time. "JoJo," they both said.

"Where is he?" Wolfe asked.

"Up the road. Pardone lets me see him, which is more than anyone else gets around here."

"That ends tonight. I have spent the last four years righting wrongs across the nation because I wanted you to be proud of me. I had to earn the right to be with you every day of my life."

She stroked his hair and ran her hand over his smooth face.

"What happened to you?" Lurleen asked.

"Sensitive to light. Hair changed color. Beard stopped growing. I'm strong and can sense radiation. Oh, and we have a daughter and a dog. They are back in Mobile, where we have a home. I hope you'll be happy if you're willing to go there."

"A daughter!" Lurleen exclaimed, smiling broadly. "How old?"

"Thirteen. She has a boyfriend named Carlisle, I thought it would be the end of me, but he is a good kid. She stayed with them while I continued to Fort Lauderdale."

"Of course, I want to go home with you. This place is hell,

but everything is better now." She took Jim's face in her hands and kissed him like a newlywed.

He started to lose himself in the moment, but then stroked her face and pushed her back.

"There will be plenty of time for that later. We cannot be caught in here. We need to go out there where I can see but they cannot. We have a lot of work to do. When the sun rises, everyone will awake to a new world, but we need help. I think there are about ten thousand women who need to be freed and turned loose on the guards. Do you know how many guards there are?"

"A hundred, maybe more. I do not know for sure. Pardone kept a lot of information from me."

"No matter. Are there any guards in the house?"

"No! He would never allow that. They were outside."

"Outside is clear," Wolfe told her. He removed the pistol from the back of his pants. "Take this. Do you remember how to shoot one?"

Lurleen nodded. "I have a plan…"

CHAPTER SEVEN

Wolfe did not want to wake the household staff, so he tiptoed while he walked. Lurleen followed, stepping quietly. Dressed in her work clothes, a long-sleeved shirt and coveralls, she looked ready to tend the cattle. The pistol in her hand told a different story.

They made it to the bottom of the steps when a voice stopped them.

"What are you doing in here?" an old woman challenged. She hurried out of the parlor, waving a mixing spoon. Wolfe squinted at her, afraid she was going to turn on a light. Lurleen touched his shoulder as she passed.

Electricity sparked through his body.

"Emmie! Mister Pardone has sent us on a special project. Very hush-hush if you know what I mean."

Wolfe could not tell if Emmie could see their weapons. He did not want to take action against the old woman, who probably managed the household.

But Lurleen was the housemaster.

"What kind of special project has you sneaking out in the middle of the night?"

"A hundred thousand pounds of beef exported this month. It is a milestone, and we are going to hang a couple banners for the work crews to share the joy and pride." Lurleen guided the old woman back toward the kitchen, where she must have been preparing the next day's food. Wolfe's stomach growled. He was not getting enough to eat.

He expected that applied to everyone except the likes of Elric Pardone. Even Lurleen had lost weight, and she was in a better position than most.

Lurleen returned and waved for Jim to follow. She went to the front door, and with well-practiced movements, unlocked it and threw it open. She walked outside as if she owned the place, maintaining the demeanor that would make Wolfe's plan a success. He needed her to act like the mistress of the manor for a few more hours. After that, all hell would break loose if it had not already.

Once outside, she scanned the area, looking for the guards. The dim lights were on but did not show much. Wolfe still had to pull his welding goggles into place.

"They were taken care of," Wolfe said softly. "They will not be sneaking up behind us, Miss Lurleen."

"I love how you say my name," she replied, pulling him close for another long kiss. His welding glasses fogged, and there was a nose print on one lens. He smiled as he took a small rag to buff it clean.

"Don't be afraid to shoot, but once you fire, there will be a lot of shooting. The lights will come on, and the world will descend into chaos. That is when we tighten the noose, but we have to be ready. Go on now. You take care of your part, and I will handle the rest."

"I will not rest until we are all free," she stated.

"And that is one of a million reasons I love you."

"I will not be afraid to shoot. Most of these men deserve to die." She smiled at her husband and headed down the access road to the women's compound, which was a veritable tent city.

Wolfe watched her go. The hard edge she had adopted had helped her survive.

And it would help her to freedom. There was a time when Wolfe hesitated to kill a man who needed killing, and the Alstons had made his life hell for too long because of it. No more. Not in this new world where the strong preyed on the weak.

God had not given Wolfe the talents he had to ignore the plight of those who could not protect themselves. His Lurleen was of the same mind.

Wolfe walked into the darkness on his way to the three guard towers overlooking the main building and the southern end of the fenced areas. They drew his attention because they were the last bastion that would prevent a wholesale escape. He needed an exit, a way out where guards would not look down on them and shoot randomly.

They did not have to kill all the escapees, only enough. Fear and intimidation were how they kept the masses under control. Wolfe wanted to remove the tools they used to accomplish that. He stalked up the road, hugging the fence to appear as nothing more than a shadow.

He could hear men talking up ahead. Turrets stood to the right and left of the access road, his goal the one on the right. From there, he had a firing line to the tower on the left and the one on the far side of the field to the right, closer to Baldwin.

The guards seemed to be engaged in a card game and were not bothering to look out. Wolfe closed on the tower. The steps led up to a gate that was locked from the inside. Wolfe did not bother going that way. There was a better way to get inside. He shinnied up one of the support legs, climbing it like a lumberjack and making short work of it.

The transition from the vertical beam to a horizontal one approached.

When he reached the high point below the tower's floor, the horizontal stabilizing beam was farther away than he'd thought. Standing on it and reaching as high as he could, the board he needed to pull himself up only brushed his fingertips. He would have to jump. If he missed, the fall was twenty-five or thirty feet. He looked for a different way.

Wolfe twisted his body through the maze of support beams and wires to get to the stairs, sliding over the rail and onto the steps. He stayed close to the rail to minimize creaks and other noises. With his hunting knife in hand and goggles in place, he tried to determine how many men were in the tower. He would have to be quick.

Only two men were playing cards. He heard a chair scrape, so they were seated. That would help. He eased up one more step to where he might get a look and heard a squeak from the stair. Wolfe bolted upward and into the tower. The two men had frozen mid-sentence. Wolfe punched one in the head and slashed at the other's throat but missed and cut deep into both arms, which had been thrown up to protect his neck. He started to scream. Wolfe plunged the knife into his abdomen, shoving upward to still his racing heart.

Two more guards were bundled up to the sides. They roused quickly with the tumult but were twisted up in their covers. Wolfe kicked one in the face, and the other held his hands up in surrender.

A dilemma. He could not leave a man behind to shoot him in the back.

"Pardone is dead. The rest of those supporting him will soon join their fat master. You have made one choice already, and that was to not fight me. The next choice you're going to make will save your life."

"I am good, Mister! Do not kill me. I am only here to work."

"Not for the women?" Wolfe pressed.

"Well, that is part of the compensation."

"Wrong answer," Wolfe replied, grabbing the young man by his throat and lifting him up until his feet dangled off the floor. "If I asked you to go to the next tower over and shoot all the men inside, would you do it if it was the only way to get your death sentence revoked? Or would you run for the hills?"

The man could not talk. Wolfe put him down.

"Do not try anything. I will kill you where you stand," Wolfe warned.

"I can do it. They only have two over yonder and two across the road here. This was the big tower."

Someone yelled from the closer tower.

Wolfe leaned over to the man in his charge. "I need you to tell him that guy was upset about losing a hand and that all is well."

He nodded before walking stiffly to the side. "Old Muff Dodger was pissed at losing a hand. He is sulking now. All is good, boss-man!"

"Keep it down, you lame bastards. We are trying to get some sleep over here," the voice replied.

"You bought yourself a reprieve. Now lay on your face."

"Do not kill me," the man pleaded.

"I will not if you do as I need you to do. I will not tolerate a change of heart. When you commit, you commit all the way. I need to do a couple things and cannot be watching you while I do them."

"Yes, sir." He dropped to his knees and slowly laid down. Wolfe watched his hands to make sure they did not go anywhere near the guards' weapons, which were now scattered across the tower. Once the man was down, Wolfe broke down the three rifles, breaking the trigger mechanisms of each so they couldn't be fired, and unloaded the shotgun. He checked the bodies, found two knives, and threw those into the fenced area below.

"Get up."

The man stood, and Wolfe handed him the shotgun. "I will toss the shells down once you are at the bottom. Go on now. The clock is ticking."

He looked at the gun and back at Wolfe.

"You've never killed a man before?"

"No, sir," he replied in a whisper.

"Here is how I am going to explain it. You took women against their will." The man started to protest, but Wolfe held up his hand. He did not want to hear it. "That is just like killing someone, but worse. They have to live with what you did. These men will not, and they probably have done the same thing as every man has here. I am putting an end to it tonight. You can be a part of the force resurrecting the dignity of those who have been put in the prison, their only crime was their gender. Go and do what you agreed to do." Wolfe emphasized his point by giving the man a shove toward the stairs.

He walked slowly.

"Hurry up!" Wolfe whispered harshly.

The man pounded his way down the stairs. Wolfe put six twelve-gauge shells into a ball cap, tied it closed with a sweaty bandanna taken from a dead man's head, and tossed it over the side.

He hung his head. Wolfe wanted to leave the man he had become right here in Baldwin, but there were more things to do. He needed that hard man to stay focused and merciless. He needed to do what those behind the razor wire could not. Without looking back, Wolfe headed down the steps. He locked the gate and climbed onto the support structure to get to the ground. It would not do to have anyone use the tower against them.

The man he let go was running west along the fence line on his way to the next security point, which was about a quarter of a mile away. Wolfe turned and took one step toward his target, the last obstacle to those coming up this road on their way to freedom. The pistol fire from the direction of the house sounded small and far away, but it was enough to alert the men in the tower.

Taking careful aim, Wolfe stitched five shots across where the two stood peering over the side, looking for the source of the pistol fire. They both disappeared from view. Wolfe ran, crossing the distance quickly, and started to climb. He shot the hasp out and kicked the gate open, continuing up. He fired randomly through the floor before sticking his head through the opening at the top of the steps.

"Come on out, and I will spare your lives," Wolfe promised. He fired where he had not fired before and rushed through the opening. The tower's occupants had died with the first shots.

Wolfe changed magazines and headed back down the tower. He started to run back toward the estate but stopped. Anyone could still access the tower. He reached into his pocket for the ever-present lighter he used sparingly and used his hunting knife to rough up the bottom of a support leg, making it like kindling. The flames did not catch readily, but when they did, they started a solid burn, slowly climbing upward. He did the same thing to the legs on the first tower.

A shotgun blast came from the direction the young man had run. It was followed by rifle fire and another shotgun blast.

The fight was on. Wolfe would deal with them later if his draftee was unsuccessful. Wolfe did not care if the man died. The hard man inside him would take a while to soften.

Wolfe started running toward the estate and on to the women's compound to join Lurleen in delivering freedom.

He pulled his goggles down and sprinted. There was no reason to delay. He needed to check the rooms where the guards were billeted, expecting them to wake and slowly stumble into the darkness.

Night was his domain.

CHAPTER EIGHT

Men were already milling around when Wolfe reached them. He counted six. He took the available cover, sticking to the shadows. Taking it easy on them would not make things easier on him. He leveled his rifle, pulled his goggles up to protect his eyes from the muzzle flash, and fired as quickly as he could pull the trigger.

Chaos erupted. Someone fired back, and then someone else. Wolfe zeroed in on them and finished one and then the next. There were a great number of rooms in the building, but some might have women in them, which took away the option of burning it down. He would have to root them out.

He ran around the side of the building to get to the power line, which was an underground cable, feeding into a junction box. He took aim and fired. The box sparked, and the lights went out. Wolfe returned to the front of the building and prepared himself to run inside. His heart raced as he opened the door and rushed through.

The tangle of arms and blows kept him from bringing his rifle to bear, and the knife was too far away, stowed in his boot as it was. He broke a wrist, making someone howl. A fist slammed into his face, and something pummeled his body.

Wolfe got a hand free and swung, hitting something solid. An arm wrapped around his face, and he bit down, drawing a yelp and blood. He started to get free when something big and heavy crashed against his head. After the lightning storm of sparks before his eyes, the world disappeared.

Wolfe awoke. He was upright, and his body screamed in agony. He could barely hold his head up, but he refused to let the men know they had beaten him. His goggles were gone, and a bonfire lit the area. He squinted as much as he could with his one good eye, seeing only vague shapes. He assumed the other was swollen shut.

He hoped that was all it was.

"You come into our house and do all of this?" a familiar voice asked. His fellow bodyguard had taken the reins of this runaway stallion. "Where is Mister Pardone?"

"I reckon he is in his bed. Why do you ask?"

"You lie!" the guard shrieked.

Wolfe had not lied. He wanted to laugh. These men had no business being in charge of anything. The business end of a rifle poked him in his bruised ribs, and he grunted with the pain.

"We are going to take our time killing you." Hoots and hollers agreed with the muscular guard. A stab of fire accompanied a thin line traced down Jim's breastbone using a small, sharp knife. The big man spat into it, bringing more pain.

Wolfe's head started to swim and he let go, giving in to the blackness threatening to engulf him.

He came to when a bucket of lukewarm water splashed over him.

Wolfe did not bother with words to drive the mob into a frenzy. He needed a bath, and that little splash was not going to take care of it. Then again, the way things were going for him, he did not expect to have to bathe again.

Another prod caused more fireworks to explode inside his head.

A soft voice called for calm.

"Get back to your building!" the big man demanded.

"No!" The combined cry came from hundreds of voices.

"Please, no one else needs to get hurt," Lurleen suggested. Her voice grew louder as she approached.

No! Save yourself. Go. Run! Wolfe's words stayed within since he was not able to make his voice work. He would have thought he was dead if it were not for the pain coursing through his body.

"There is no need to threaten anyone. Elric Pardone is no more. He succumbed earlier this evening to the effects of avarice and vice."

"Say what?"

"We can talk together about the way forward for the farm and the business. A lot of good work is done here."

"And we will keep doing it the same way. That is how it gets done!" a man from the crowd shouted. Wolfe could not tell how many were in each group but figured the men were outnumbered a hundred to one. His head rolled back and forth as he tried to look up but failed. Too much pain. Too much weakness. He closed his eyes to focus his mind and body on healing enough that he could die with dignity.

The blast from in front of him shocked him back to the moment.

Through a squinted eye, he saw Lurleen stoop to pick up

the rifle with her free hand. The other held the pistol she had fired into the guard's face.

She called a name, and a woman hurried forward to take the pistol from her.

"Any others out there want to dispute my authority?" She waved the rifle toward the crowd of men, looking for one with enough backbone to stand up to her. Her finger was on the trigger since she was willing to kill any man with the guts.

None challenged her. "Good. It is time for y'all to leave. Your rooms are forfeit. We will need you to depart the premises immediately."

Lurleen raised the rifle in the air and fired a couple of rounds to speed up the process. Without her saying anything, other women cut Jim loose. He collapsed.

"Thanks, honey," he mumbled before passing out. Lurleen collected his goggles before they were trampled and looked for help to get her husband to the house.

CHAPTER NINE

Wolfe woke in a big bed. It was cool and dry, so the room had air-conditioning. He tried to get up, struggling against the pain. He managed to get one more pillow under his shoulders and fought to get his breath back, tired after that little bit of work. He rested his head against the headboard and fell back asleep.

It was dark when next he roused to consciousness. He wondered about the time, even the day. Nothing seemed real. A glass of water was on the nightstand. He sat up, having an easier time of it than before. A bathroom was outlined by a pale night light that beamed as bright as the sun. Wolfe could not find his welding goggles, but he was able to see out of both eyes. That provided limited relief. However long he had laid there, the swelling had gone down.

The bathroom seemed too far away, but he had to go. He had slept enough to build up the energy. He swung his legs off the bed until his feet rested on a throw rug. He slowed his breathing.

"Jim?" The voice of an angel came from the other side of the bed. He had not even noticed that he was not alone.

"It is. Finally." He tried to turn around, but the twisting hurt his chest too much. Lurleen jumped out of bed and rushed around to his side. He looked up at her. "I have never seen a lovelier vision."

She smiled and carefully kissed his forehead, then bent down so he could drape an arm over her shoulders. Lurleen lifted as she stood until Jim was on his feet.

"You have lost weight."

"A little," he admitted. "You, too. What about JoJo?"

"He is getting big. We're going first thing in the morning to get him."

"I will be ready," Jim promised.

"You will not. You are busted up pretty bad. We have a nurse who took a look at you. You need to take it easy and let your body heal before you go anywhere. When I said we, I meant me and about two thousand more women. We have all the weapons. We are going for our kids, and no one will stop us."

"Be home in time for dinner," Wolfe joked while stepping gingerly toward the bathroom. He was tired of complaining about the pain, which was less than before but still excruciating. He was with Lurleen! He wasn't supposed to be in pain.

He stopped and caressed her face with a single finger. All the agony of the last four years had been worth it. He took a deep breath, wincing from the stabs of his tortured rib cage, and continued into the bathroom. Lurleen left him to take of business.

She waited outside the door. "Will you cut my hair like you used to?" he asked.

"Of course, sugar plum. Anything you want. Anything."

He did not reply. That was how it used to be. She had agreed for him to become a truck driver because the pay was good. He wanted her to have a nice home and nice things, but when the world ended and none of those things mattered, he hadn't been where he needed to be. She had only agreed because she'd thought it was what he wanted.

Wolfe had liked driving the truck, but his motivation was Lurleen.

"I will not leave you again," he told her.

"I expect not, Mister James Wolfe. We are a family, and we are going to live together. I will not have any other situation, not under my roof."

The simple act of flushing a toilet mesmerized him. Here were Lurleen and Jim, joking and having fun just being with each other. People lived a lifetime and never experienced anything as simple as the enjoyment of being in the presence of the one who made them whole.

"I married a strong woman. You make me proud of who I am and proud of you."

Lurleen did not answer. Her eyes glistened and sparkled.

She helped him back to the bed, where he settled back in, exhausted from the simple act of being helped ten feet and back.

"Sleep well, darling," he mumbled. "And tomorrow, you get our boy and bring him back to me. I want to tell him about his sister."

"I want to hear about her, too. Get some sleep, Jim. We have to take a trip to Mobile when this is all over. You will need your strength."

He was asleep by the time she finished speaking. She stroked his white hair. It was growing on her, as if she were married to her very own rock star.

CHAPTER TEN

In all the world, the Baldwin compound was now the safest place for women, and they aimed to keep it that way. The men's barracks had been burned to the ground. There were too many bad memories in there for it to survive. Rebuilding would start with tearing down.

It continued to smolder, leaving a sliver of smoke trailing skyward. The guard towers had been torched. The men's weapons had been taken, and the men had been chased away unless one of the women spoke for them and no one spoke against.

All that happened the First Day, a new holiday for Baldwin. It was the day Jim Wolfe hovered on the edge, close to being in a coma as his body struggled with the horrific injuries inflicted by men whose lives had run their course.

The women had taken their vengeance. Very few had left the camp under their own power. New signs were placed, declaring that any former guards would be shot on sight. New armed guards stood by the gates, allowing entry to honest tradespeople and shippers. Others who had taken advantage had already learned to stay away. The men had run far and wide that first night and taken word of the uprising with them. Their fear was enough to encourage others to seek their fortunes elsewhere.

That left a fully functioning cattle farm in the hands of the Collective, the consolidated women owners, who handed out equal shares to all members. The administrative team worked with new zeal, striking the lists of the guards and other male overseers and replacing them with the new owners. Work still had to be done, but the workers would be paid for their labor. They were also free to leave. The choices were theirs, and they could make the decision whenever they wanted.

It was the dawn of a whole new day.

Then came Second Day, the day they reclaimed their families.

Lurleen dropped the magazine into her hand, checked that it was fully loaded, and popped it back in, racking the slide to the rear to chamber a round. She slipped the pistol into a jacket pocket before running Jim's AR-15 through the same check. She had never fired that particular model, but she knew the basics. She loaded a round in the chamber and checked the selector lever to make sure it was on safe.

"Let's go get our kids!" she yelled at the mass of bodies swarming around the estate house, then turned and strode boldly up the road on her way to the interstate. They had a six-mile walk in front of them, and only those who could make it there and back in one day were going along.

A few wagons with concerned citizens were waiting on I-10. If anyone struggled, they could ride for a while, or they would carry those with small children on the return trip if they chose to return.

It was a new world, and no one was ordering them around. It was amazing to see what they would do when they were asked. They believed in the Collective. They embraced hope.

Like making a twelve-mile round trip. There were less than a thousand children at the facility, but two thousand volunteers went to get them. Get all of them, even if they could not match children with their parents.

There was another hurdle they would have to cross later. The older children had disappeared, and no one knew where.

It was a mystery that those with older children had vowed to solve. They were armed and had no intention of returning to Camp Baldwin until they knew the answer.

They took a shortcut to the interstate, climbed the hill to get to the main roadway, and settled into a good pace to get there in less than three hours. Everyone was used to hard work, so the walk was not a trial. New scenery and animated conversations brightened their spirits.

The group took a break after the second hour and drank what water they had before continuing. Lurleen was one of the few women who had been there before. She knew the way and led them unerringly. They passed an executive airfield on their way to the converted warehouses and pseudo-playgrounds.

The excitement within the group grew, and many started walking faster. They were getting close, and the tension was palpable.

Lurleen held up a hand for the women to stop. Some started to run, but others yelled at them. The journey to get their kids was about to get hard.

A roadblock had been put into place up ahead. Maybe it would stop the wagons, but not people on foot. Then again, maybe it was not about stopping people from walking through.

It bristled with men carrying guns. Some dropped behind the barrier and aimed over the top. Lurleen looked back at the group. The women were not going to give up, but getting themselves killed would not help their families.

"Does anyone have a white rag?" she called.

One was rapidly passed to her. She tied it around the rifle's barrel, then thought better of it. Lurleen handed the AR-15 to a hard-looking soul who said she could shoot.

Lurleen picked three women to go with her and they started to walk, going slowly, hands in the air, waving the white towel.

She stopped when she was close enough for the men to hear her.

"Pardone is dead. You need to let us through to pick up our kids. We will be out of your hair in two shakes of a lamb's tail."

"Still work to be done, and they are the ones doing it." One man stood up to be the designated mouthpiece.

Lurleen kept her companions from raging forward.

"Thank you for your candor, but that is not going to work for us. We need our kids. No one in their right minds keeps families apart."

"We do," the gruff voice answered.

"You know that you should not. We will get our kids, and we will be on our way."

"No can do. Now piss off."

"That is not how cultured Southerners talk. If you have any influence over our children with manners like that, I shudder to think how they will turn out," Lurleen countered. The women snorted at the comeback, but it suddenly became intensely hot, standing in the middle of the roadway.

Sweat started to roll down Lurleen's forehead. She glanced left and right. The others felt it, too. This was not what they had expected. Lurleen had hoped their numbers would carry the conversation and the men would back off.

But they were not and gave no hint of being impressed by the mob before them.

"Come on, now," Lurleen coaxed. "We cannot stand out here all day. There are cows to milk and cattle to butcher. It is not getting done while we are here."

A shot rang out from behind her and hit the roadblock's speaker in the chest. He fell backward and was still. The men shouted and started to fire indiscriminately toward the mass of women. Lurleen ran for the ditch, diving as rounds impacted all around her. Two of the women with her were down. The other rolled into the ditch beside her, eyes wide and breath ragged from near-panic.

Rifles fired as fast as they could, brass starting to cover the pavement on both sides of the roadblock.

Lurleen crouched and ran down the ditch toward the roadblock.

"Where are you going?" the other woman cried. Lurleen did not bother answering. She was on a mission. JoJo was on the other side of these men.

She refused to let them stand in her way.

The brush caught her clothes and scratched and cut her skin, but she ignored it. She was able to get past the men. She peeked from the side of the road. One man stood tall behind the others, his arms crossed.

Cut the head off the snake, Jim had said.

She skulked around behind the man, trying to control herself as those firing their weapons hooted with each hit on one of the women.

Lurleen jammed her pistol into the middle of his back. "Tell them to stop firing," she said coldly.

"They do not work for me."

"Yes, they do. Give the order."

"Hey, fellas, cease fire," he said conversationally. One of

the shooters turned. Lurleen did not want there to be any doubt.

She wrapped a slender arm around his neck and pressed the pistol to the side of his head. "He said, cease fire!" she shouted.

A woman's voice from behind them got their attention, even if they did not hear the exact words. One turned, and then another, tapping each other on the shoulder to let them know. They stood and faced her. At least they were no longer shooting into the crowd. Lurleen made the mistake of looking past the roadblock at the bodies littering the pavement.

She felt like she'd been slapped. "Put your guns down, gentlemen."

They made no move to comply, so she bounced the pistol barrel off the leader's temple, hard enough to make his knees buckle. She did not let him fall.

"Put them down," she reiterated.

Once the first had placed his rifle on the ground, the others quickly followed. The leader started to struggle, grabbing her wrist in a vice-like grip.

Lurleen wasted no time in pulling the trigger. The .45 caliber round blew through his head as if going through a watermelon, and she let his lifeless body fall to the ground. She had no need for bravado. Her ears rang from the explosion so close to her face.

A man lunged at her, and she shot him in the chest. He continued to stagger forward and fell to his knees before her. She reared back and kicked him in the face.

"Anyone else?" Maybe these men needed bravado to keep them from getting themselves shot. She shouted toward the women, "Can I get a hand, please?"

Some jumped up and started running toward the roadblock. The first to arrive collected the weapons and passed them out to the women. They pummeled the men with their bare fists, but Lurleen would not let them execute the shooters.

"Stop!" she shouted to get their attention.

The Collective held the men on their knees before Lurleen.

"You are not laughing now," she said. "Is it no longer funny, gentlemen? We came to get our kids, and by God, we are going to do just that. Eileen, I think these men need to dig the graves for those they killed. Maybe we will even let them use shovels."

Lurleen walked away. The children's area was a quarter-mile ahead. She wondered if the women would get the same reception by the children's camp guards. She would do what she had to. She was beyond caring about the sanctity of the lives of her and her son's captors.

CHAPTER ELEVEN

A large contingent of women herded the roadblock shooters back to the bodies. It was Florida in the late summer, so the dead and dying could not be left in the open for long. The men crumbled quickly when forced to look at the faces of their victims. Whether it was a real change or a temporary act did not matter. They had a job to do.

"There is a small gravel pit about a quarter mile that way. We can put them there," one suggested. "May we use the wagons to transport them?"

Anger was high. Many said no, but calmer heads said yes. They loaded the wagons but left nine dead behind, making the men carry one of the bodies each, walking with them over their shoulders as if they were on the way to Mount Calvary.

With all the wagons engaged, they were able to convey all the bodies in one trip. Many of the observers cried in silent vigil. They still had it in them to feel and to care. Lurleen stopped her march to the front gates to watch, bowing her head as the wagons rumbled away with the trudging men following. She did not expect to see the men return.

There was so much anger. The pressure cooker had blown its top, and there was no way to get that pressure back inside. The only thing they could do was gather up the children and disperse to establish a new equilibrium.

Lurleen had other ideas, too, about the future for the Collective and Camp Baldwin. That would come soon enough if the rest of the owners cooperated.

The mass of women renewed the march, fifteen hundred strong after five hundred were killed, wounded, or taking care of those who were. They walked with their arms locked together and filled the roadway from ditch to ditch, row after row.

Armed guards stood at the closed gates, looking through the slats and wires of the children's fortress.

Lurleen saw female faces looking back at her. Taken aback, she hesitated before saying, "We are here for our children. Please open the gates and let us collect them."

"We have to keep this area secure if we do not want our own children taken. I'm sorry," one answered sadly.

"Those who would take them are no longer in a position to do so. Look at us! We have broken the chains. Elric Pardone is dead. His henchmen are dead. It's time to rebuild. Join us. Get your kids, and let us go to a new home. It may look like the old home, but it is completely different," Lurleen explained, approaching and touching the woman's fingers as she leaned against the slats.

"We still have guards in here. Nothing is different."

"Let me talk to whoever is in charge," Lurleen pleaded.

"Yes, ma'am," the woman replied.

"It's Lurleen. We are all equal now. Your masters have come to the end of their days."

Lurleen reached behind her to feel the comfort of the pistol. She hoped she would not have to use it again. The adrenaline rush was starting to wear off, and her anger had faded to the point where she simply wanted it all to be over.

When a heavy-set man approached, the anger rushed back in a tidal wave. He was all too familiar.

"Aren't you my brother's whore? Go back to his bed where you belong." He sneered.

A collective gasp rolled from the crowd behind Lurleen. She casually pulled her pistol. He started to laugh, and she shot him in the face.

"No one calls me that. No one calls any of us that. Not ever." She put the pistol into her waistband and turned her attention to the woman behind the gate, who was staring in shock at the body. "If you would be so kind as to open the gate, we would like to go about our business."

"You killed Mister Pardone!" she blurted.

"Yes. Anyone else needs killing? We can take care of that first, so our children do not see it," Lurleen explained.

The second woman at the gate unlocked it while the first remained frozen. She tried to pull it open, but the body was in the way. She kicked him in the head, then again, and then again. The gate would not move.

They needed the help of a few friends. The crowd behind Lurleen surged forward, pushing the gate that had caught on the Pardone brother, and dragged his body away from the opening.

Lurleen stopped to talk to the first woman. "Recover your wits, lovely lady. We have work to do. The sun will set on a new world that you will be part of shaping."

"Will it?" she asked. "Will it be a new world, or is this another chance to get my hopes crushed?"

"I assure you, the Pardone family is short three members. Their influence has run its course. It is our time now. Grab your kids and come with us." Lurleen took the woman by the hand, even though she wanted to run in and find JoJo.

"Are your children in here?"

The woman shook her head. "They are at home."

"My son is in here. Come with me to find him, and then we'll go get yours."

"I think I'll go home now. Baldwin for a new life?"

"Camp Baldwin for a new life. A new opportunity. A new world."

"Trading one master for another?" The woman remained skeptical.

"That is something we will talk about as part of the Collective. Everyone works for someone, but does everyone work for someone who cares about them doing a job they appreciate? It is a high hill we have to climb, but one that is open to us, when it wasn't only two days ago."

The woman sat down.

"Good luck," Lurleen told her and backed away before turning toward the building.

JoJo was somewhere inside. Once she was on her own, Lurleen raced in, eyes darting here and there. She passed crying mothers hugging their children, women with frantic looks, and confused children wondering what was happening.

Lurleen passed a male guard holding a rifle. He made no move to stop anyone. "I'll take that rifle, please."

He handed it to her without saying a word. She took the rifle and slung it over her shoulder.

She hurried through the area, adding her voice to the many calling out names. JoJo was still too small to work in the factory. Or was he? It had been a month since she had last seen him.

The workshop where they turned fabric into clothing was up the road. The children did not have to do a great job. In the post-war world, any clothing was good clothing. They only needed to use their small fingers for the fine work, and the bigger children used sewing machines. And when the children got older?

Lurleen did not know what happened to them. She wanted to find out because she knew mothers who deserved to discover where their children were.

Like she wanted to find JoJo at that moment. She searched through one area after another, asking as she passed, holding her hand just above waist-high to show how tall her boy was.

None had seen him.

A large group of those who came but did not have children stood away from the others, giving them space to reunite. "If you've found your children, please move outside the gate," Lurleen called.

Others picked up the call until a parade of families strolled toward the gate and out. Lurleen clenched her jaw and steeled herself as children looked for mothers who were not coming. Other women swept them up to give them the attention they craved.

It was heartbreaking.

The liberated women had become a well-armed militia to right the wrongs of the past. The pendulum was swinging.

"I need a few of you with me. We need to check the facility next door where the factory is located."

Too many women joined her, but she did not complain. They headed out the back gate on their way to an immense building.

CHAPTER TWELVE

The warehouse gates stood open. No one was around.

"Oh, no! Lurleen cried and started to run. The mass of bodies broke into a sprint. The door to the warehouse was locked, and she looked at the two women behind her. "Wait here."

She waved for others to follow as she looked for another way in. Down the long side and around the corner, all doors were locked. There was no fire escape. Although it was a tall building, the second floor did not have an outside exit.

The back side held two doors, one to an unlocked equipment room. The other was secure, so they walked around the far side and back toward the front. Three locked doors later, she found herself back where she'd started.

"Did they lock themselves inside?" someone asked.

"Looks like it," Lurleen replied.

Another shoulder-rammed the door, but Lurleen stopped her from making a second attempt. She pointed to the hinges. "It opens outward." She stared at it for a moment. "Who has a knife?"

A couple appeared. She took the bigger one and worked the hinges until they slid free. Using the knife as a pry bar, she jammed it into the space between the door and the frame on the hinge side. It started to move, but it was an all-steel door and heavy.

"Stand back. When this thing starts to fall, it will not care who is in its way. And be ready with those guns, but do not shoot. We got kids in there."

"I'll do it," a slight-framed woman said, holding out her hand for the knife. "You are better with a gun."

Lurleen nodded and stepped back. She reached for Jim's AR-15, but she had not gotten it back from whoever she gave it to earlier. She did have the guard's weapon, and she checked it quickly—a hunting rifle. Simple to use with a round in the chamber.

The small woman leveraged her body weight, getting the door started and guiding it away from the frame when it came free. The lock came with it, and it started to fall. She pulled her hands away and stepped back. Lurleen pointed the rifle and stepped into the semi-darkness, moving to the side to let others through.

"The Pardone family is dead, and the guards who survived are running away as fast as they can hightail it. We have come for our children. We will take them and leave you be," Lurleen shouted.

A shot rang out, hitting the woman standing in the door-way. Her only crime was trying to see into the facility, looking for her son.

Someone fired back.

"No shooting!" Lurleen yelled. She started to be able to see in the darkness. When she'd moved aside to let the others through, she had gone behind a barrier. Luck had kept her alive. Sometimes that was what someone needed. She slung the rifle and took out her pistol, then peeked around the corner and saw the cheap barricade with only two defenders. Behind them, the children had been corralled into the center of the space, where four others held them in.

The area behind the two at the barricade was clear. Lurleen braced the pistol against the vertical barrier, a massive support stanchion. She took careful aim and fired, adjusted, and fired again. Both men went down. She crouched and ran to the barrier, which was little more than overturned tables.

"Walk away now, or we will hurt you in ways you cannot imagine," Lurleen shouted at the other four.

"We got your kids!" a bold voice countered.

"What are you going to do with them? I suggest the answer is 'nothing' unless you wish to be dismembered slowly. The last sound you hear will be yourself screaming and crying. You know the only way out is through us, which means you need our permission. Send all the children to us, and we will let you walk out the back door." Lurleen had never expected to be in an episode of a crime thriller, but here she was.

She now better understood the tortured characters on the TV screen and the lengths they were willing to go because they had hit a point where they could no longer be coerced as people in a decent society might. She had already demonstrated a level of violence she had never known she possessed. She could see that her husband had hit that point long ago.

Let evil have its way, and all suffer. Standing up to evil unleashed a power that made her afraid of herself and what she had become. She wanted JoJo back, and she wanted all the children turned loose. Lurleen was using her anger for a good cause.

Or was it a selfish cause? People needed clothes. They needed food.

She clenched her teeth so hard her jaw started to shake. People needing those things did not mean that others should lose their right to live free. The power of righteousness gave no one authority over others.

Lurleen handed her pistol to the woman next to her and stood with her hands raised over her head. A different approach was needed. She could not abide anyone hurting the children.

"This fight is over." Lurleen slowly walked forward. "Every person you know is dead or running for their lives. Which side of the ground do you wish to wake up on?"

"We all die in the end, lady."

"And the entirety of our lives is spent in delaying that inevitable conclusion," Lurleen drawled pleasantly. She lowered her arms, crossing them in front of her chest and giving the men her "mom" look. Had it been light enough, they would have seen the bloodstains on her clothes, none of the blood hers. "Go on. Get out of here while you can. You know the things you have done, and so do we. Go someplace else and start fresh. Clear your consciences however you can."

"Who said there is anything wrong with my conscience, lady?"

"Lurleen. My name is Lurleen. JoJo, are you in here?" She still had not seen her son and wanted to know that he was there.

"Mom!" a voice cried from the middle of the group.

"Thanks for telling us who we need as a hostage to guarantee our safety." The conscience-free man laughed.

Lurleen looked over her shoulder. "Get people to all the exits. If they try to leave with a hostage, kill them."

There was a rustle and stamping feet as many of the group ran to do as Lurleen had asked.

"We brought two thousand, and your window to do the right thing is closing." She took a deep breath and yelled, "Hide, JoJo." The man had made her mistake clear.

Her hard side warred with Lurleen's good side. If she had kept her pistol, she would have rushed the coward, even though he carried a scattergun. His fellows did not appear to be convinced that taking a hostage was a good idea.

"You might want to talk him out of it," Lurleen tried looking from one anxious face to the next.

He peered at the mass of children, pressing tightly together to prevent the man from pushing in to take any of them. The bigger kids on the outside had locked arms. Tears came to Lurleen's eyes. There *was* good in the world. It only took one to start the ball rolling.

"Forget this, Billy Ray. I am out of here."

"You stay put, or you will have me to deal with."

"We stay put, you will be the least of my problems." He stuck his chin out in defiance, then placed his shotgun on a table and walked toward Lurleen with his hands up. "You said you would let us go."

"Let this one go. No hostages, and they walk free."

The muttering from behind her suggested some did not feel the same way as Lurleen. She turned and stormed back toward the doorway.

"Have you not had enough killing?"

One woman with a rifle looked down, brow furrowed with anger. "No," she admitted.

"It is okay to be angry. Hell, we all are. We are here to get our kids back and end this. The healing starts right now, but that is not going to happen with more killing. We have to live with whatever we have done. Maybe they do not have consciences, but I know we do."

She held her rifle out, and Lurleen took it.

"Let him go and make sure he keeps going."

"There is no doubt about that, ma'am. You will not see me again."

"And such are the words that give us hope," Lurleen said. The mass parted and he walked through, his fingers clasped on top of his head. Once past the glares, he started to run without looking back.

Lurleen strolled back. Two more put their guns on the table and walked out with their hands on their heads.

"Looks like it is down to you and me, lady." He raised his shotgun slowly, taking aim. Lurleen dove out of the way and rolled behind a worktable. He snorted.

The kids charged, tackling him. The shotgun blasted into the floor, spraying pellets and sending women diving for cover. The children hammered on his back, kicking his arms and legs and head. Lurleen ran to the pile of bodies.

"*STOP!*" she yelled and started pulling people off him. "You do not want to be like him."

She picked up the double-barreled shotgun. One shell was unfired. She snapped it closed and nudged his groaning face with the business end of the barrel.

"Go find your moms," she told the kids. JoJo pushed through the group to wrap his arms around her waist and hold on. She ran her hand over his head. "Your daddy has come home. He is alive!"

"Dad?" JoJo said, confused.

"Yes, your daddy is alive. He got hurt pretty bad freeing me and everyone else, but your daddy is waiting for us to return. We have so much more to tell you, but later."

"Touching," the man mumbled as he worked his way to his feet. A small group who had not found their children at either location loomed nearby.

"Can you take care of this thing?" she asked the women,

handing the shotgun to one as she walked past them on her way outside with a protective hand wrapped around her son's shoulder.

The shotgun blast from inside the building did not come as a surprise.

CHAPTER THIRTEEN

After a call to those who had gone around the building to wait at the doors to recover all their children, the group started to gather and stroll down the road. Stragglers joined them amid shouts of joy and hugs of support for those who had reunited their family.

The wagons had finished their gruesome task and waited on the road with the captives from the earlier fight bound and sitting nearby.

Lurleen looked for someone willing to interrogate the men and found a soul she had spent the first year with. They had supported each other through the darkest of times. "Betty Jane, would you please talk to these individuals about where the older children have gone? They need to give you good answers. Otherwise, you are free to do to them what they have done to us."

The woman waved a broomstick. "I have the perfect tool for the job."

"Wait! I'll tell you everything!" A young man came forward, and none of the others tried to stop him.

"You are making this too easy. Why should we believe you?"

"Because we were wrong. *I* was wrong. I will tell you even if you are going to kill us because that is what we deserve."

"Tell us," Betty Jane prompted.

"They were taken to Jacksonville to work the fishing boats. They took the bigger kids because the job required more strength. I can lead you to them."

"How many guards are there?"

"A hundred, maybe more," he said softly.

Betty Jane looked at Lurleen. "We can take them, but not right away. We will need a plan."

"I know just the person." Lurleen nodded. "We will return to Camp Baldwin, and when we are ready, we are going to Jacksonville."

Betty Jane agreed. "What about them?" She stabbed a thumb in the men's direction.

Lurleen turned to them. "Are you with us?"

The young man nodded vigorously. The others seemed less committed. "If we take care of them now, we will not have to do it later," Betty Jane offered, shaking her rifle suggestively.

The men came on board quickly after that. "I am with you!" one man shouted as if he had just found Jesus.

"Bring them to Baldwin. A six-mile walk in the sun will weed out the unbelievers," Lurleen replied. She guided JoJo toward the center of the road. With her son in tow and her husband waiting, she did not expect the walk to take long.

CHAPTER FOURTEEN

"Take it easy. Your daddy is injured," Lurleen whispered. She had already told JoJo about the changes to Wolfe's eyes and hair. He tiptoed to the side of the bed and coughed heavily into his hand.

Jim Wolfe dragged the goggles over his face before he opened his eyes. "Who is this little man?" he asked, poking a finger toward his son's chest.

"Dad!" It was the cry of all youngsters when their father tells a bad joke. Lurleen sat on the edge of the bed, enjoying the moment they were reunited as a family.

"I hate to say it, my loving husband, but we have a problem, and we need to go to Jacksonville."

"I feel a lot better. I am ready to go," he replied, wincing as he tried to sit up.

"You are not, Mister Jim Wolfe. You will stay in bed until you can move without crying out in pain." Lurleen had taken over. Jim was not about to argue.

"I know you are right. I have had to take care of myself for too long and had too many others counting on me to rest when I was hurting."

"I fear you will not be completely healed before we have to go, but we need you to plan the recovery of the older kids. Your ability to see in the dark makes you uniquely suited to show us how to get inside, close to the kidnappers. We will take care of it from there."

Wolfe shook his head but did not say a word. He could not take his eyes off his six-year-old son.

"You have a sister now," Jim said.

"Do I have two moms?" he asked. Jim and Lurleen smiled at each other.

"No, it is not like that. I found her on the way here. She had lost both her parents, and I needed someone to look after that big dog of ours."

"We have a dog? Can I see him?" JoJo beamed with excitement.

"They are both in Mobile. We will go as soon as we take care of this other thing. I will not leave until your mother is ready."

"And that means we need a few more days before we can go," Lurleen said. "Come on, sweetheart. Let us see how everyone is getting on. We have a cattle farm to run."

Jim leaned forward to give his son a hug, then slid his legs off the bed and sat up. "I am coming with you."

Lurleen wanted him to come but did not want to stress him.

"We will walk slow for you," JoJo said.

"That is my boy. Slow is good. I'll come back if it hurts too much, but I do not see how I can feel anything but good right now."

It took two days, but Wolfe's incredible strength healed him far faster than a normal person. He felt solid as he buttoned up his gear and checked his backpack.

"We could ride," he suggested. "I have my bike."

"You went to the house and got your bike?" Lurleen put her hands on her hips and looked at Jim sideways.

"I went to the house looking for you," he explained. "The bike helped me get here more quickly. I will tell you the sordid details of my extended journey when we are on our way to Mobile. I would offer to go get Jennifer and Buddy and bring them back here, but I remember quite well the last time I left home to go do something."

Lurleen chuckled while shaking her head.

"You are not going anywhere without us."

"Ever again," he agreed. "I love hearing you laugh. I had forgotten what it sounded like. When we go to Jacksonville, all of us are going. You too, JoJo. Are you ready to be a man?"

"I am," the six-year-old solemnly stated.

"Uh-huh," Lurleen grumbled.

"I hid my bike a couple miles away. I'll go get it and be right back."

"I thought you just said you weren't going anywhere without us?" Lurleen crossed her arms.

"We will do without the bike. JoJo can walk ten miles without a problem."

JoJo puffed out his chest, and Jim ruffled his hair.

"Is the army ready to march, General?" Lurleen asked with a smile.

Jim hung his head. "The last time I went to war against an armed outfit, we lost some good people, but we also freed an entire town and removed the boot heels of those who would hold them down. Come tomorrow morning, I expect we will be able to say the same thing. And yes, the troops look ready to march. How is the ammunition?"

"Minimal," Lurleen replied. "Many of the guns only have a few rounds, but we have shared what there was and loaded what was left. We have more than enough to defend ourselves, but if they start any real trouble, we may have problems."

"I think you are the general, not me. A man cannot lead this army, but I will walk by your side." The two looked at each other like newlyweds.

Wolfe left the house first so he could hurry ahead and stand with the others as Lurleen emerged holding JoJo's hand. He started clapping and the others joined him, a few at first, then all five hundred. She eyed him suspiciously. He rolled his finger to encourage her to make a speech.

She held her hands up for quiet while JoJo gripped her leg. Jim hurried up the steps to lift his son onto his shoulders before retreating to the group to be an observer.

"One last trip to recover our own. Will it impact the fishing industry? Yes, but that is their issue, not ours. We are going after the rest of our children, and we will do what it takes. I hope there is no bloodshed. That is also in their hands. My husband can see in the dark as well as you, and I can see in the daylight. His special ability means he will be able to check the docks in the middle of the night where no one will see him. He will conduct the initial look-see tonight and first thing tomorrow morning, we will let them know that we have arrived."

Lurleen had said what there was to say. She walked down the steps and took her husband's hand as they headed for the highway for the walk to Jacksonville. They'd stop at a location they had selected to camp, based on what the cooperative young man had told them.

He was coming with them, but the other men from the barricade shooters were not. They had been taken in a wagon about twenty miles west of Camp Baldwin and dropped off. If they returned, they would do so at their own peril.

The Collective's army settled in for the long hike, walking more quickly than they had with greater numbers on the first round a couple of days prior. A few more good meals under their belts and a grim determination to deliver justice added fuel to their fires.

Plus, they took comfort in knowing the farm was in good hands. A former manager, a nurse, and a veterinarian had been nominated to keep the farm producing and shipping their products, and they had transitioned to new management without a hiccup. The Collective had been formed and was running. The workers were motivated to do the jobs, and a larger portion of the meat had been allocated for feeding the new employees.

The women who had been working in the office continued to work there, but they no longer had to look down since they no longer had overseers. They kept the records with which the others could make business decisions. The trade would continue, but the benefits would no longer flow to a small number who never got their hands dirty.

Peace of mind lightened the loads of those heading on the final recovery mission. Once the older kids returned, housing, schools, and an entire community would have to be established. The women were up for the task. Some had lived in the tents for nearly four years. They were ready for a change.

"Do you like to fish?" Jim asked.

"I do not know," JoJo replied.

"We used to go when you were a toddler. When we get to Mobile, we will go fishing, maybe even go out on a boat. I used to work on a commercial fishing boat, and the captain was a gracious man, agreeing to bring me to Fort Lauderdale so I could look for you. But we beached in a bad storm north of Tampa. My friends survived but remained behind to fix the boat. I hope they did and were able to get back home to Mobile. They are good people. There are a lot of good people out that way. They even have restaurants."

JoJo shook his head. "What is a restaurant?"

"There is a lot to learn about this world. Going out for a meal used to be common, but now it is a treat."

"It was always a treat for us, darling," Lurleen said.

They continued talking about everything, making the walk go quickly. After three hours, Wolfe asked Lurleen to pass the word for everyone to walk in silence. With the help of a woman who had lived her whole life in Jacksonville, they took side streets to avoid being seen. It was still early in the day. Too early.

They continued slowly for another two hours until they closed on St. John's river.

They found an area to hide five hundred people, settling them into the shade. "I will scope the docks with Miss Nora. The boats should be at sea, but processing and transport will be waiting for them to return. The guards should be less than vigilant unless men from the labor camp made their way here to raise the alarm."

Lurleen kissed him goodbye with a fierce passion that demanded he return, and he *was* coming back. He had no desire to take unnecessary risks. Jim had a family to support, and they supported him. That made him smile.

Nora, the woman who had guided them along the side streets, led the way to a point where they could see the new fishing docks. The entire operation had moved to the north side of the river in the center of downtown Jacksonville. Before the war, it would have made no sense to put the oper-ation downtown because shipping was not a problem and commercial space was at a premium. When the vehicles had stopped running, it was easier to move the food to the people.

"What about the bombs? Did they not land here?"

"Everything east of here is gone because of a direct hit on the naval station. This fishing facility is for the river and the lake only, but there are plenty of fish to feed those who are left. That young man said they tried a second smaller operation in Saint Augustine, but ocean fishing is a problem because a bomb hit nearby, so the water is spoiled."

"We had problems in Mobile," Wolfe said. "But they overcame the challenges by installing steam engines to drive the propellers. We did not have polluted water out that way, even though the bombs landed on all sides."

"How many bombs fell?"

Wolfe shook his head. "Big ones and small ones in numbers too great to count. There are entire areas out west that are toxic in Idaho, Utah, and Colorado. Every state I have been through had Hot Zones."

Nora pointed at the river. "A fishing boat right there, and another. They do not seem too adventurous about going downstream."

"We are looking for hundreds of kids. They have to be somewhere."

Wolfe saw small boats with one or two teenagers each.

Nora led the way forward, sticking to the shadows. More people appeared on the roads and streets, none of them armed. Wolfe broke his rifle down and stuffed the two halves into his pack, then tucked the pistol into the back of his waistband.

Nora had to hide her shotgun. She took out all the shells in case someone was watching her from one of the many smoked windows overlooking the area. If they came out and stole the shotgun, they would not be able to use it. The

Collective had other twelve-gauge shotguns, but there was no other ammunition.

The two moved into the open to walk past many former corporate buildings on their way to the new wharf.

"Bold move, Jim," Nora whispered.

"We will not go so far that we cannot get out." That had been Wolfe's idea, but a plan was taking shape, and it required a bold move. He did not want this fight to drag out. He preferred to end it decisively in one quick stroke while the enemy was split, half at sea and the other half in port.

Wolfe grabbed Nora's arm and pulled her sideways, hurrying behind a building. "What did you see?" She looked confused. Wolfe pointed up. She leaned her head around the corner and looked up. Rifle barrels poked out from under the umbrellas atop a low-roofed building.

"I think we found our guards," she muttered. "We could blow it up and be done with them."

Wolfe looked at her through his dark welding goggles. "Do you have any explosives? I was never much into blowing stuff up and do not have the faintest idea how to go about it."

Nora shook her head. "We could burn it," she suggested.

"We need to get a better look at who else lives in that building. If the children are held there, we will have to root out the guards one by one." Wolfe headed around the steel and glass structure they were hiding behind. In back, there was a window broken out, and he climbed through. Probably a thousand others had gone that way over the years. Rats and refuse littered the bottom floor.

He looked for the stairway and thought he found it, but the access door was secured in some way.

Wolfe pulled on it, using all his strength. It gave, and the metal of the handle ripped through the steel of the door, then he yanked it open and headed in. It had been secured for a long time. He was the first one in there, it seemed, since the place had not been scavenged. He started climbing. It got dark in a hurry, and he was able to remove his goggles.

"Wait here," he told Nora. He reassembled his rifle and handed it to her. "Kill anyone who tries to come up after me."

She preferred the alternative of blocking the door, and she sat on the steps to wait.

Wolfe ran upward. On the top floor, he slid his goggles back into place, left the stairwell, and looked for the side of the building facing the one where they had seen the guards. He approached the window wall in a crouch to look down on the shorter building far below.

He scanned the entire area. Inland from the docks, he saw what looked to his trained eye to be a fish-processing facility. People milled about—little people. The number was not in the hundreds, but it was a start, and that was only what he could see.

Guards with weapons were in and around the building, a former hotel, and scattered around the docks all the way past the processing facility. From what Wolfe could tell, the guards were both men and women. He went to the other sides of the building to see if there were any more concentrations of people with guns but saw none. He was concerned about a line of wagons waiting for the freshly cleaned fish to move to smokers for long-term processing or directly to cookpots to feed a hungry population.

Once he decided on his plan, he had to act. They would not be able to get it done quickly, but he reasoned that time was a commodity that was easier spent than lives. The sooner they started, the sooner they would be able to pull the trigger and free the kids. As long as they knew where the children were, they could slowly close the noose around the facility.

Wolfe headed back downstairs.

Nora opened the door and shrugged. They had had no visitors.

"How often did you eat fish in Camp Baldwin?"

"Two or three times a week," she replied.

"Then they will know you have thrown off your chains."

"We had fish three days ago, after Pardone and his thugs died. The next shipment is probably due today."

"I do not want to disappoint the good folk at the farm. Whatever we do, it will be after the wagons leave. We can move people into place ahead of time. My first thought was to conduct two attacks because the guards were split, but I am not sure how many are on the boats. Almost none, I think, because there are far more with guns out there right now than there should be. We will let the boats return and the wagons depart, and then we will see where the children go and what else is in the guard building."

"And after that?"

Wolfe smiled. "Then we will hit them where it hurts the most."

CHAPTER FIFTEEN

Wolfe explained the plan to twenty of their people, who shared it with the rest. He and Lurleen walked among the women to ensure they understood what they were supposed to do. Jim had kept it as simple as possible since he thought that would be the most effective.

A complex plan would break down quickly.

It was late afternoon before Nora led them out. It was important that they be in place when Wolfe gave the signal to act. He looked down at JoJo. He and Lurleen were going to the battle, and they were bringing their son.

"Please stay down, and keep him down, too," Jim whispered to Lurleen. She nodded tightly, and he kissed her. "I know you want to play a role in freeing the children, and you are. You are here, and you are doing the right thing. I will take care of it for you both, and I will not be far away."

She tried to nod but ended up dipping her chin to her chest and looking down. "So much anger," she mumbled. "I am tired, Jim."

"I am, too. Hold on a little bit longer." He held her for a moment before they had to catch up with the group.

Five hundred walked in silence, dropping off in groups of thirty in locations where they would be able to catch the guards in a crossfire. Thirty rifles and shotguns would be ready to fire from ten different angles, and two huge groups would liberate the children from the processing stations once the fishing boats returned.

Wolfe hoped they would get back around the same time. That was not critical to the plan but would be an added bonus. He did not want to hang around any longer than necessary. Like Lurleen, he simply wanted to go home. It was a long way away, but it was almost within reach.

These men and women were standing between him and spending quality time with his family. He started to get angry, just angry enough to heighten his senses and improve his reflexes. He could feel it.

Jim put Lurleen and JoJo with a group in the big building kitty-corner from the guards' hotel, then slid out the back and joined the group hiding in the shadows between the docks and the hotel. The area bustled with activity, which was exactly what Wolfe wanted. They had taken long enough getting back that most of the berths had boats in them, and the presence of more people in the area indicated they had just arrived.

Between Nora and the young man, they were able to get the first eight groups into position. The last two were trapped behind the wagon train that waited patiently for the fish to be delivered.

Teenagers loaded wagons like they had in Mobile using shovels. The first one was already maneuvering to get out, the driver expertly guiding his horses while the next wagon in line moved up.

From what Wolfe could see, six more waited. The last two hundred women hunkered down, staying out of sight while

Nora peeked through overgrown bushes. She called out the status a moment later.

"Children are going into the next hotel over between the guards and the docks," Nora reported quietly.

"How many adults with guns are going in with them?" Wolfe wondered.

"I do not see any." She moved her head back and forth to get the best view through the bushes. "There are guards stationed on the corners to watch them go in. There are probably more guards at the entrance, but they are leaving the children alone."

She did not add that the children hung their heads as they walked, a combination of being tired and defeated. They did not bother looking around. They had lost all hope.

One wagon remained when a new stream of children came from the processing area and headed toward their hotel. The guards on the corners watched, making sure the children did not go astray. Two of them singled out two young girls and pulled them aside. The two struggled briefly but quickly gave up.

Wolfe's blood boiled. There had been a time when he minded his own business, but that was well past.

"Execute the plan," he told Nora and stepped out of the bushes on his way toward the two guards.

He jogged toward them, hurrying before they disappeared. "Excuse me, gentlemen," he said evenly.

They looked at him strangely, not used to being interrupted. "Are you new?"

"I am. Jim Wolfe and I am here to take these two with me."

"Like hell," the one said. "I will need to talk to Mister Davis."

"He sent me. He is busy," Wolfe bluffed as he continued to approach.

"You can stay right there," one said and started to raise his rifle. Wolfe lunged, lifting the barrel of the rifle and driving it into the man's face. Wolfe took the weapon from him as he fell and swung it like a club at the second man's head. On impact, he went down like a sack of bricks.

Wolfe crouched to look the girls in the eye. "Tell me where the guards are and how many? We are here to free you. We brought your mothers," he told them. They stared at him blankly.

He left them and walked to the corner to look around it. As Nora had thought, two men with rifles stood in the shadows by the front door. The two girls nearly walked past him before he stopped them. "Wait here."

He did the same as before, walking like he had a purpose on his way toward the front door. One held out a hand to stop him. "Mister Davis sent me," Wolfe said casually.

"Okay," the second said and stepped aside. Wolfe started to walk between them, then reached out and grabbed their heads, pulled them inward, and smashed them together. He was still angry, and that made him stronger. Two crushed skulls later, he let the bodies drop and walked inside. No one was there. The reception area was vacant, and the first-floor hallways were clear.

He strolled to the back door on the opposite side of the lobby, where he found two more guards outside. Wolfe walked out, surprising them, and nodded politely before punching the first in the throat, then kicking the other in the knee. The leg twisted with a crack and the man fell, but he hung onto his rifle.

Wolfe stomped hard on the man's groin, and he let go of his rifle. Wolfe picked it up, along with the one from the first man. With a quick snap of his boot, he knocked the second man unconscious, a good thing since he seemed to be writhing in agony.

"I cannot have you sneaking up behind me," he told the man.

Wolfe walked across the open area toward the new docks where the boats were tied up. The abandoned pylons formed an ad hoc dock across from a real dock next to a full private marina that had been pillaged, leaving sunken boats blocking the entrance. The high-rise condo tower overlooking it had suffered a horrendous fire. Scorch marks stained the walls, and the windows had blown out from the lowest to the highest levels.

Most of the boat captains ignored him. Only adults were around the boats, which made it easier.

Wolfe walked onto the dock. "I need y'all to get off your boats and come onto the dock."

The closest captain gave him the finger, followed by a string of invectives. Wolfe looked behind him to make sure the women were in place, raised his rifle, and squeezed three rounds into the air.

At the count of ten, nearly two hundred guns fired at the same time.

"Please do not make me ask a second time. You see, the guards are no longer needed, and they will not be coming to your rescue since they are probably dead. However, you gentlemen serve an important purpose in today's society. I would rather not kill you, but if I have to, I will. We can find someone else to drive your boats."

The cursing captain retrieved a rifle from the wheelhouse and came back out on deck. Wolfe aimed and snap-fired a single round through the man's chest, but it was enough. He glanced quickly at the others.

"Now we are short one captain. How many more drivers are we going to have to find?"

The others finally overcame the shock of things being different and left their boats to stand on the dock.

"You, what is your name?"

"I am Captain Tom," he replied as if Wolfe should have known that. He pointed to his grubby shirt, where a patch read Tom.

"Well, Tom, I am going to need you to take the weapons off each boat and bring them to me. Holding them by the barrels, of course."

"I do not have a rifle on my boat," he declared.

"We can verify that in a little bit." The women's rifles fired a second time. After that, only a few scattered shots rang out before a long silence.

"It appears that we have cleared the riffraff out of the fishing industry," Wolfe noted.

Tom brought the rifle that Wolfe had already seen and laid it on the deck. He quickly went through the other boats before holding his hands up. "That is all I could find."

"Well now, that creates a bit of a dilemma. I do not believe you, Tom. I think there is a weapon on each boat, and for every weapon I find, I will kill its captain. It will be your fault, Tom. I will kill you last for lying to me."

"I have one under the bench," a grizzled old sailor stated.

"Go get it, Tom." Wolfe stared at him until the captain complied. "By the barrel, like I told you."

He handed it over and continued to the next boat, looking at the captain for guidance on where to look for his weapon.

"Fine. It is in the cabinet. Just an old scattergun I use for ducks if I can find them."

Wolfe nodded. Tom dutifully removed the weapons from each boat, including his own. Wolfe unloaded them, stuffing the shells into his pockets before he tossed the weapons over their heads and well toward the center of the river.

"Get up and come this way. We need to meet up with the others." Wolfe backed off the dock onto dry land and took a position where he could funnel the captives toward the hotels. They trudged past him, glaring but complying with his orders.

Nearly two hundred women had swarmed through the processing facility, sweeping up every child within to stand on the riverside. Wolfe tipped his head to them. They formed a barrier for the boat captains, leaving them only one way to go. The women draped arms over thin and narrow shoulders.

If looks could kill…

When the captains encountered the women, their pretense of being outraged ended. The men bowed their heads as they passed.

"Continue to the guard building. If anyone is left alive, they will be your fishing crews. If you do not have any volunteers, you will have to ply your trade by yourself."

When they reached the space between the two hotels, they found the guards standing outside without their weapons, their wrists bound. Teams of women were running through the children's hotel, telling everyone to pack.

Evening was closing in.

Wolfe turned his charges over to a detail that had lost their humor a long time ago and found Lurleen and JoJo. She was at the front of the group, getting ready to talk to the guards who had surrendered.

"I think we'll need to stay here tonight. Did we lose anyone?" he whispered.

"We did not, and here is fine. They surrendered quickly after the first volley, thank goodness." She nodded with a slight smile, touching his arm gently. He took JoJo's hand, and Lurleen walked forward.

"Your reign has ended. The Pardone family is dead. As soon as we find Mister Davis, his time will end, too."

She walked back and forth in front of the twenty-odd

guards who had been stripped of their weapons, many sporting black eyes and bruised faces.

"We need the fishing industry to continue. The boat captains are here."

"Minus one," Wolfe interjected.

"Most of the boat captains are here," Lurleen corrected. "You can hire on with them and take up commercial fishing. The need for food is as great now as it has ever been. The source of labor, however, will have to be you and not slaves. The children are coming with us, and if you were thinking about following us, we have all the guns now, and as you saw, we know how to use them.

"We will stay here tonight, and since we cannot trust you, we are going to have to lock you up somewhere. I hope you do not mind the temporary inconvenience you will have to suffer through for one night. We will leave in the morning, and you can figure out how you are going to keep the fishing trade alive. Otherwise, you starve, but that will be your choice and not someone else's."

Nora stepped forward. "We saw a banquet room in their hotel. We can put them in there and provide guards all night. Probably tie them up, just because."

A terrifying scream came from above, a balcony near the top of the building. A man fell, and he hit the ground with a sickening thud.

"Suicide?" Nora asked.

"People don't scream when they jump on purpose," Lurleen replied, based on what she had learned watching television back in the day. "I wonder if that was Mister Davis?"

Nora shrugged. The team going through the guards' building was cleaning house. Random shots concerned Lurleen until a woman waved from where the man had fallen.

"Get them out of here." Lurleen hugged Nora. The two women bumped foreheads as they looked past the pain into the good souls behind each other's eyes.

Lurleen faced the crowd of women and bigger kids. "You do not have to work the boats and fish processing anymore. You are all going with your mothers if they are here, and if not, then you will go with us. We will take care of you, and you will not be forced to work."

One young man raised a hand. "But I want to stay," he said. A couple others nodded.

"Is there an adult to take care of you, and I do not mean these guards?"

"He is my dad." The teenager pointed at one of the boat captains. His voice sounded young.

Lurleen scowled. The young man had been swept up from the fish processing facility and looked much like the others. "Go to your dad," she conceded.

"We need to find the kids some dinner and get set up for the evening," Wolfe said. Lurleen tapped him on the shoulder.

"They have this part under control," she said softly. The reunited families walked away, almost as if touring a college campus. The children without parents were descended upon to ensure they were looked after. One of the two girls Wolfe had saved came up to him.

"I am sorry. I need to thank you for what you did. It came as a surprise. No one does something for anyone else around here. Well, not the adults," she added sadly.

"Not anymore. We are here for you. Is your mom here?" Lurleen asked.

"I do not think she survived. I take care of myself, and I am not doing a very good job of it." She tried to smile through greasy strands of hair.

"It looks like your friend has found hers."

"Yes, and they asked me to go with them. Should I?"

Wolfe stood tall. "I cannot answer that for you. This is your chance to make a decision for yourself. It is an important one, but if you wish to talk about it, we will help you—Lurleen, JoJo, and me."

She nodded and walked away, heading toward her friend. She had not taken long in deciding what to do.

"How are you doing?" Jim asked.

"I am fine. I feel safe for the first time in a long time," Lurleen replied with a tired smile.

"I know where there are some fishing poles," Jim told JoJo. "What do you say we throw a couple lines in the water and see if we can catch anything?"

JoJo brightened and looked at his mom. "Can I?"

Lurleen. "We are all going fishing." They strolled casually toward the docks, while the rest of the group they had brought from Baldwin took care of everything else.

CHAPTER SIXTEEN

The walk back to Baldwin took most of the day after the final liberation. They stopped to eat twice because most of the children were undernourished, just like the adults. They did not make good time, but they eventually arrived.

Jim, Lurleen, and JoJo stopped by the admin building to tell the workers the good news. The leadership team had hurried downstairs and was waiting for them since they had been watching the road and saw the group arrive.

"You got them!" Alice Main cheered. She had moved into the lead position because of her experience. She had been one of the managers of the facility before the bombs fell.

"We freed all that were there, and just as importantly, we did not lose anyone." Lurleen was proud of that.

"You will have to tell us all about it tonight while we have a massive barbecue. We will butcher two cows for this momentous occasion to welcome the kids back the right way." Alice clapped Jim on the shoulder, grinning at the announcement. Jim turned to Lurleen.

"And then tomorrow, we will be on our way. We have a home in Mobile," Lurleen explained, smiling at her husband.

"You are welcome at Camp Baldwin anytime. We will keep the lights on for you."

"Will you be able to keep the windmills and solar panels working?" Jim wondered.

"As well as we can. We have quite a few engineers here, good people who came from Huntsville, Alabama. I think they look forward to getting back to work on the stuff they're good at instead of shoveling cow manure. We have all had a lifetime of practice with that." The woman chuckled.

"I am glad we can laugh. It feels like a different life that happened decades ago." Lurleen gestured toward the door. "We will clean up and get ready to join you."

"We have moved some people into the big house since it is now our hospital, but we kept your room as it is. We will convert it after you are gone, but you will always have a bed in Baldwin."

Jim shook his head. "And that is how tourism will return —one punchy sales pitch at a time."

JoJo stayed with the ladies in the admin building while Jim and Lurleen ran down the road to get the bike. She jogged slowly, but it was only a couple of miles away. Jim did his best to remember where he'd put it.

They had been given a cart to pull behind the bike, using a leather strap that wrapped around Jim's waist. It was not optimal, but it would save Lurleen, and most especially JoJo, from having to walk to Mobile, which was around four hundred miles away. The cart waited in Baldwin, along with two spare cans of gas. It was not surprising, given the amount of equipment and materiel stored and staged on a farm of Baldwin's size.

They ran easily, Jim keeping pace with Lurleen to cover the distance in twenty minutes or less.

"Halt right there!" a voice shouted from the trees.

Jim held out his arm to stop Lurleen and push her behind him.

The man stepped into the open, sporting a pump shotgun.

"Seth. You found your gun," Wolfe commented.

"You! So that is what you look like."

Wolfe kept his hands on top of his head while watching every one of Seth's movements. "The world has changed since you have been gone. I believe the farm will have work for you, but it will not be what you are used to doing. And if you abused any of the former residents, well, you will have to answer for that."

"I had a pretty good life. Eldon made sure that I was taken care of," Seth admitted

"Then you will want to be on your way, going in the other direction as fast as your legs can carry you," Wolfe advised.

"I recognize you," Lurleen stated coldly.

Jim understood her tone. His AR-15 was strapped across his back, but he had left everything else at the farm. They were only going to be gone for a half-hour. He missed his pistol.

But he had his hunting knife. He let his hands drop slowly. "We need to talk about this. The time for dying is done. It is now time for living."

"You have it backward, Mister. I was living before. I am dead now." He kept the shotgun pointed Jim's way. Lurleen pushed out from behind Jim to stand at his side.

"Our son is waiting back at the camp. We are finally together. You seem like a decent sort. Let us go back to our family and be on your way before you take this past where you can't get yourself out."

"Mine is the permission you need. Let me think about that." Seth scratched his chin, and an evil smile spread across his face. "You come with me," he pointed at Lurleen, "and your man can go back to your son. He only needs one parent."

Lurleen had no intention of going anywhere with Seth.

"You know I will do what I have to do to survive," she said in a low voice and strode proudly to the young man. He lost his smile and stared. When Lurleen reached him, she grabbed the barrel of the shotgun with both hands and shoved it straight up in the air.

Jim pulled his knife and charged, and his unnatural speed helped him close the distance in half a heartbeat. He drove the knife into Seth's exposed belly so hard that he severed the spine. Wolfe withdrew his bloody fist and let the man collapse.

Seth's jaw worked, but he only managed to gurgle. Lurleen cracked the shotgun and showed Jim two empty chambers.

"That bluff cost you your life." Jim took the shotgun and broke it in half, then tossed both parts into the wetlands beside the road. He bent down and wiped his hand on a clean spot on Seth's clothes.

He started walking, talking to Lurleen over his shoulder. "The bike is just up ahead." He glanced at the dying man in the middle of the road. "I gave you a chance."

"I think you gave him two chances, but that is how people are nowadays." Lurleen sighed. "Will we ever look back on this and worry that our souls are condemned forever because of the amount of killing we have done?"

They continued walking while Seth died a slow and painful death.

"I do not think killing evil men will stand us in good stead with the wrong people. We do what we have to do. I gave people a chance, and they failed me. Again and again, they chose strength over kindness. They found out how strong I am, how strong you are, except in Mobile. *They* only offered a hand in friendship. I hope you like our new home."

"I cannot wait to see it. You said your motorcycle is up here? I will be good if I do not have to walk four hundred miles."

"Me, too," Jim agreed. He thought he recognized the turnoff, headed in, and plowed through the brush into the backyard. He held his breath until he could see his motorcycle was still in the shed. He rolled it out, brought it back to the road, started it up, and motioned for her to get behind him, but she had a different idea. She lifted his arm from the handlebar and straddled his lap to kiss him in a way that promised much more.

He killed the engine and flipped the kickstand out so he could love his wife right there in the overgrown yard, chasing away bugs and beetles with a swatting hand.

But that did not matter. They were together again after all those years. Everything that had happened in between was quickly becoming a distant memory. So much had changed, but one thing had never faded – the light within their souls burning for each other.

Two days later, Wolfe slowed the bike, braking easily so the strap around his waist, securing the bars from the wagon behind him, did not throw him over the handlebars. He turned off the engine and parked the bike, then undid the strap and let it drop to the ground. He was stiff from driving.

Lurleen and JoJo were just as stiff from riding, despite the cushion of blankets.

Someone peeked out the window before throwing the door open and running down the stairs.

Miss Jennifer almost made it into Wolfe's arms before Buddy raced past her and bowled into him.

"Dog!" Jim stumbled back before reaching over the furry animal and hugging his daughter to him. JoJo started petting Buddy and received a lick on the hand for his efforts. "Miss Jennifer, this is Lurleen and JoJo."

The End
Nightwalker Book 8

Wolfe has had a great run, but all things must come to an end. I appreciate you sticking with us for Frank Roderus' *Nightwalker* series. Follow the series here: https://geni.us/Nightwalker

If you like this book, please leave a review. Your opinion matters to me. Plus, reviews buoy my spirits and stoke the fires of creativity.

Don't stop now! There's more…

AUTHOR NOTES - CRAIG MARTELLE

Written June 5, 2020

You are still reading! Thank you for continuing to the end. I feel like I just finished *Nightwalker* 7, and I did, but in between, I wrote *Judge, Jury, & Executioner 9* and *Bad Company 7*. That was over 200,000 words in those two books. Add in the two *Nightwalkers*, and we come to nearly 265k words in about seventy-five days. The story machine is cranking.

So much has happened in the past couple of months. Quarantine, Isolation, all trips canceled, wearing masks everywhere, and now civil unrest. So much that demands our attention. And still, at the end of the day, we have stories that need to be told.

We have legacies that need to be stocked, like Frank Roderus' legacy. And mine. In the case of *Nightwalker*, ours are intertwined. In a good way, we forge ahead.

Needless to say, with the world shut down because of COVID-19, I had plenty of opportunities to observe what happens when things start to get out of hand. It is a telling indictment of what has become of humanity, and also what happens when groups have too much power over other groups.

But *Nightwalker* ends with hope, freedom, and a bright future. We do what we have to in order to survive, and then we make the rest of our lives worthwhile. That makes it all worth it.

Peace, fellow humans.

Please join my Newsletter (https://craigmartelle.com – please, please, please sign up!), or you can follow me on Facebook since you'll get the same opportunity to pick up the books for only 99 cents on that first day they are published.

If you liked this story, you might like some of my other books. You can join my mailing list by dropping by my website www.craigmartelle.com or if you have any comments, shoot me a note at craig@craigmartelle.com. I am always happy to hear from people who've read my work. I try to answer every email I receive.

If you liked the story, please write a short review for me on Amazon. I greatly appreciate any kind words, even one or two sentences go a long way. The number of reviews an ebook receives greatly improves how well an ebook does on Amazon.

Amazon – www.amazon.com/author/craigmartelle

BookBub – https://www.bookbub.com/authors/craig-martelle

Facebook – www.facebook.com/authorcraigmartelle

My web page – https://craigmartelle.com

That's it—break's over, back to writing the next book.

ABOUT THE AUTHOR

Frank Roderus wrote his first story—it was a western—when he was five. It was really awful, as might be expected, but his mother kept that typed and spell-checked short story tucked away until the day she died.

Later, Frank became a newspaper reporter, thinking that books are written by authors which he most assuredly was not. He kept trying to write though, and eventually did it wrong enough to learn how to get it right. That first sale, a young adult novel published by Independence Press, was more than thirty years and a good many books ago.

As a journalist, the Colorado Press Association awarded Frank Roderus their highest award, the Sweepstakes Award, for the best news story of 1980, and the Western Writers of America has twice named Frank recipient of their prestigious Spur Award.

Frank passed away at age 73 in December 2015.

BOOKS BY CRAIG MARTELLE

Craig Martelle's other books (listed by series)

Terry Henry Walton Chronicles (co-written with Michael Anderle) – a post-apocalyptic paranormal adventure

Gateway to the Universe (co-written with Justin Sloan & Michael Anderle) – this book transitions the characters from the Terry Henry Walton Chronicles to The Bad Company

The Bad Company (co-written with Michael Anderle) – a military science fiction space opera

Judge, Jury, & Executioner (also available in audio) – a space opera adventure legal thriller

Shadow Vanguard – a Tom Dublin series

Superdreadnought (co-written with Tim Marquitz)– an AI military space opera

Metal Legion (co-written with Caleb Wachter) (coming in audio) – a military space opera

The Free Trader – a young adult science fiction action-adventure

Cygnus Space Opera (also available in audio) – A young adult space opera (set in the Free Trader universe)

Darklanding (co-written with Scott Moon) (also available in audio) – a space western

Mystically Engineered (co-written with Valerie Emerson) – Mystics, dragons, & spaceships

End Times Alaska (also available in audio) – a Permuted Press publication – a post-apocalyptic survivalist adventure

Nightwalker (a Frank Roderus series) with Craig Martelle – A post-apocalyptic western adventure

End Days (co-written with E.E. Isherwood) (coming in audio) – a post-apocalyptic adventure

Successful Indie Author – a non-fiction series to help self-published authors

Metamorphosis Alpha – stories from the world's first science fiction RPG

The Expanding Universe – science fiction anthologies

Monster Case Files (co-written with Kathryn Hearst) – A Warner twins mystery adventure

Rick Banik (also available in audio) – Spy & terrorism action adventure

Published exclusively by Craig Martelle, Inc
The Dragon's Call by Angelique Anderson & Craig A. Price, Jr. – an epic fantasy quest

For a complete list of Craig's books, stop by his website – https://craigmartelle.com